No Time
For Love

Barbara Cartland

No Time For Love

Thorndike Press • Chivers Press
Thorndike, Maine USA   Bath, England

This Large Print edition is published by Thorndike Press, USA and by Chivers Press, England.

Published in 1999 in the U.S. by arrangement with International Book Marketing Ltd.

Published in 1999 in the U.K. by arrangement with the author.

U.S. Hardcover   0-7862-2029-5 (Candlelight Series Edition)
U.K. Hardcover   0-7540-3866-1 (Chivers Large Print)
U.K. Softcover   0-7540-3867-X (Camden Large Print)

The text of this Large Print edition is unabridged.
Other aspects of the book may vary from the original edition.

Set in 16 pt. Plantin by Al Chase.

Printed in the United States on permanent paper.

British Library Cataloguing in Publication Data available

Library of Congress Cataloging in Publication Data
Cartland, Barbara, 1902–
    No time for love / Barbara Cartland.
        p.   cm.
    ISBN 0-7862-2029-5 (lg. print : hc. : alk. paper)
    1. Large type books.   I. Title.
    [PR6005.A765N6 1999]
    823′.912—dc21
                                                    99-30988

No Time
For Love

Chapter One

1904

Larina Milton, walking up Wimpole Street, remembered that the Barretts had lived there.

Instantly her imagination carried her into the sick-room where Elizabeth Barrett had lain year after year thinking she was an incurable invalid.

Then suddenly Robert Browning had come into her life and everything was changed.

> "How do I love thee? Let me count
>   the ways,
> I love thee to the depth and breadth
>   and heighth
> My soul can reach."

Larina quoted the lovely words and wondered if she would ever feel like that about a man.

'Supposing,' she thought, 'a man like Robert Browning appeared now at this moment and asked me to go away with him to Italy? Would I accept?'

The idea made her laugh, then she thought she would never have the courage that Elizabeth Barrett had shown.

She gave a little sigh.

"There are no Robert Brownings for me," she told herself. "I have to be practical. I have to find work."

Her mother had so often chided her for day-dreaming, for letting her imagination carry her away from the mundane affairs of everyday life into a fantasy world where she could forget everything else.

Work! Work!

The word seemed to repeat itself over and over again in her mind and she knew it was going to be difficult.

Women of her social position did not work; they sat at home with their parents until they got married; then they kept house having plenty of servants to do the menial tasks.

But those were women, or rather ladies, who had money, and a sudden fear of the future made Larina tremble.

She had known they were spending their last penny on her mother, but nothing had mattered except that she should get well.

But even money had failed to save Mrs. Milton, and when she died Larina's whole world crashed around her.

She had not even contemplated during those long months in the Sanatorium what it would be like when she was alone.

She had been buoyed up with the hope that her mother would live, convinced that her prayers would be answered, optimistically confident about the future.

It had been a Fool's Paradise, another fantasy from which she had been brought back to earth with a bang.

Deep in her thoughts Larina realized that she had walked past the number she was seeking, 55, and she had already reached 73.

She turned back to retrace her steps, and once again almost irresistibly she thought of Robert Browning walking as she was, up Wimpole Street, towards the Barretts' house.

There would have been a look of excitement on his face and he would have walked quickly because he was so anxious to be with Elizabeth again.

> "— I love thee with the breath,
> Smiles, tears, of all my life! — and,
>   if God choose,
> I shall but love thee better after
>   death."

Elizabeth must have written that, Larina

9

thought, because death was always very near her and therefore inevitably in her thoughts.

How could she be so sure that she would survive death? How could she know that wherever she might be she would still be thinking of Robert and loving him?

There was no answer to this question and now Larina had found number 55 and was walking up the steps with their iron railings on either side of them.

She stood looking at the door in an ugly shade of dark green, with its heavy brass knocker and wide-mouthed letter-box.

'It is a waste of money for me to come here,' she thought. 'It is sure to cost a guinea, perhaps two, and I can ill afford it.'

She hesitated.

Should she go away?

She felt so well, there could be nothing wrong with her. But Dr. Heinrich had made her promise that when she had been home for a month she would have herself examined by Sir John Coleridge, physician to the Royal Family.

"There is, I believe, absolutely no danger that you might have contracted tuberculosis from your mother," he had said in his broken English.

"I kept to all the precautions which you

insisted upon," Larina replied. "I have never been with the other patients, except out of doors."

"You have been very good, Miss Milton," Dr. Heinrich approved, "an exemplary visitor, if I may say so. Very unlike some of the relatives who often make my work very difficult for me."

"I shall always be grateful for your kindness to Mama," Larina told him.

"If only she had come to me sooner," Dr. Heinrich said with a sigh. "It upsets me, Miss Milton, more than I can ever tell you when I lose a patient. But in your mother's case, her lungs were far too infected when she arrived here for my treatment or for even the magnificent air of Switzerland to effect a cure."

"Mama was quite young," Larina said almost as if she spoke to herself. "I thought that would tell in her favour."

"It would have," Dr. Heinrich replied, "if she had come to me at least a year sooner. Then I should have had a hope of keeping her alive."

He paused and then he said:

"I am going to be frank with you, Miss Milton, and tell you that your mother did not help me as she should have done. If a patient has the will to live, if he or she stubbornly clings to life, then that is often far more effective medicine than anything a Doctor can prescribe."

"Mama missed my father so desperately," Larina answered. "They were so happy together. She told me once that losing him was like losing half of herself. She felt she had nothing left to live for."

There was a little throb in her voice which made the Doctor say in a different tone:

"Now we have to think about you. Have you any idea what you are going to do?"

"I will go back to London," Larina replied. "After my father died my mother leased a small house in Belgravia. It has been let, but it is actually free at the moment."

"I am glad to hear that," Dr. Heinrich said. "We have all grown very fond of you, Miss Milton, and I did not like to think about you alone with nowhere to go."

"There is no need to worry about me," Larina answered with an optimism which she did not in fact feel.

At that moment however she had no idea that all the money her father had left had been spent. That was a shock waiting for her when she arrived back in England.

"There is one thing I want you to promise me," Doctor Heinrich said.

"What is that?" Larina enquired.

"A month after you have been home in London you will consult my friend, Sir John Coleridge, and get him to give you a check-up. I shall take every possible test before you leave. At the same time, let us be frank, you have been living for nearly twelve months with people who are all infected with what we have to admit has been an almost incurable disease."

"Surely they will find a cure one day for consumption?" Larina cried.

"There are experiments taking place all the time," Dr. Heinrich replied. "I may say without conceit that the most successful treatment up to now has been my own. It is not always looked on with favour by my more orthodox colleagues but a number of my patients leave here with improved health."

"Everyone speaks of you in the most glowing terms."

"At the same time I have my failures and your mother unfortunately was one of them. That is why you must promise me that you will be overhauled not only in a month's time, but again in perhaps six months."

He saw Larina's expression and added:

"I do not want to frighten you. There is, I am absolutely convinced, virtually no chance that you could have caught consumption from your mother or anyone else, but in my experience precaution is far better than cure."

"I promise!" Larina said.

"Sir John will tell you after his examination when he wants to see you again and you must do as he tells you."

Larina nodded.

It would, she thought at the time, be very ungracious and ungrateful of her to argue with Dr. Heinrich after he had been so kind.

Because her father had been a Doctor, Dr. Heinrich had taken her mother and also herself at very cheap and generous terms which the other patients in his expensive Sanatorium might well have envied.

Little though it was, it was more than they could afford; but whatever it cost, it had been the only chance Mrs. Milton had of survival.

With an effort Larina put out her hand now towards the bell on the right hand side of the door. As she did so she saw there was a notice above it which read:

'Bell out of order — please knock.'

So instead she lifted up the heavy brass knocker and gave two rat-tats on the door.

For a moment there was no sound. Then

she heard footsteps on what she guessed was a marble floor and a moment later the door opened.

She had expected to see a servant, but instead a man wearing a conventional black frock coat stood there. He had a high stiff collar and a well-tied black cravat in which there was a tie-pin consisting of a large pearl.

"I have an appointment with Sir John Coleridge," Larina said nervously.

"You are Miss Milton? I was expecting you. Come in."

"Are you Sir John?"

"I am!"

Larina entered and closed the door behind her.

"My secretary has gone out for her luncheon," he said, knowing she must think it strange that he should open the door himself, "and the servants are ill with influenza, a fashionable complaint at this time of the year!"

"Yes, yes, of course," Larina said apprehensively.

Sir John led the way across the Hall into a room which looked out onto the back of the house.

It was a typical Doctor's consulting-room and all too familiar to Larina.

There was a big, impressive, leather-topped desk, with a hard, upright chair in front of it. A couch against one wall was half-concealed by a screen, and a book-case was stacked with medical tomes.

There was a table with a number of un-identifiable instruments on a clean white cloth.

"Sit down, Miss Milton," Sir John said, seating himself behind the desk and opening a folder which contained, she saw, a letter from Dr. Heinrich.

Sir John picked up a pair of spectacles and placed them on his nose, then lifting the letter read it carefully.

"Dr. Heinrich informs me that your mother has died of tuberculosis," he said. "He has asked me to examine you to make sure there is no chance that you have con-tracted the disease."

"Dr. Heinrich examined me before I left the Sanatorium," Larina said, "and every test was absolutely clear."

"That is what he says in the letter," Sir John said with just a note of reproof in his voice as if she had anticipated what he was about to tell her.

"I am sorry to hear that Dr. Heinrich could not save your mother," he remarked after a moment.

"He did everything that was humanly possible," Larina replied.

"And who should ask for more, even from a Doctor?" Sir John remarked. "Very well, young lady, undress behind the screen. You will find a garment you can put on. Then lie down on the couch and let me know when you are ready."

Larina did as she was told.

She took off the plain, inexpensive gown she had bought before she went out to Switzerland and laid it over the chair which stood beside the couch.

Her petticoats and underclothes followed.

It did not take long, and she slipped her arms into the shapeless white linen hospital-gown which was lying at the end of the couch.

"I am ready!" she said as she lay down, her head on the small hard pillow.

Sir John walked with heavy footsteps across the room and pushed the screen aside so that there was more light from the big window.

"You are nineteen, I believe, Miss Milton?"

"Nearly twenty," Larina answered.

Sir John had already inserted the ends of his stethoscope in his ears, so it was doubtful if he heard her.

'Nearly twenty!' Larina thought to herself. 'I have done so little in my life and I have so few qualifications.'

The only thing she could really say in her favour was that she read a lot.

Her father had encouraged her to read the books which interested him and were mostly on ancient civilizations and, as her mother often pointed out, not much use when it came to living in the world today.

"Instead of learning about the ancient Greeks and Romans," Larina told herself, "I ought to have been studying shorthand and learning how to type."

The large, noisy typewriters she had seen in offices and which had been used by her father's secretary were a complete mystery to her.

Now she thought how foolish she had been not to take the opportunity of at least trying to understand how it worked.

She had been just seventeen when her father died and was still having lessons with teachers who came to the house.

"I am not going to have a Governess living with us," her father had said firmly. "And I do not approve of girls going to school and getting independent ideas. A woman's place is in the home!"

It would have been a very nice idea, Larina thought to herself, if she had a home to be in.

"Turn over, I want to listen to your back," Sir John's voice said.

She did as she was told and felt the stethoscope against her skin.

'I wonder what this is going to cost me,' she thought. 'It is just a waste of time and money!'

"You can dress now, Miss Milton."

Sir John moved away from her pulling the screen back into position as he did so. Larina got down from the couch and started to put on her clothes.

She wore a very light corset. There was no need for her to have tight laces with which to pull in her waist. It was in fact less than the standard eighteen inches.

But she was well aware that the rest of her figure from a fashionable point of view was much too thin.

"You must eat more, darling," her mother had said to her in Switzerland. "Do you really think such long walks are good for you?"

"I cannot just sit about doing nothing, Mama," Larina answered, "and I love walking. The mountains are so beautiful and I only wish you could come with me along the paths through the woods. They have so much mystery about them. They make me think of all the fairy-tales I have ever heard."

"How you used to love them when you were a child!" Mrs. Milton had replied with a smile.

"I remember you reading me a story about the dragons who lived in the very depths of a pine-wood," Larina answered, "and I still believe it!"

Her mother had laughed.

"You belong to the sea," she said. "That is why I called you Larina."

" 'Girl of the Sea'," Larina had exclaimed. "Perhaps I have an affinity with it, I am not sure. We have never been to the sea long enough for me to find out. Here I feel I belong to the mountains."

"As long as it is not too boring for you, my dearest," Mrs. Milton had murmured.

"I am never bored," Larina had answered and it was the truth.

She put her hat on her head and fastening it securely with two long hat-pins she pushed back the screen and walked across the room to where Sir John was sitting at the desk.

He was writing on a piece of foolscap and she saw her name at the top of it.

"I have something to tell you," he said, "which I am afraid you will find very distressing."

"What is it?" Larina asked.

She felt as if her heart had stopped beating and that every nerve in her body was suddenly tense.

"You have not contracted the disease which killed your mother," he said, "but you have in fact only three weeks to live!"

Going back to the little house in Eaton Terrace, Larina could not believe that she had actually heard Sir John say the words.

It seemed as if her mind had ceased to function and she told herself that what he had told her was impossible to believe as the truth.

As she journeyed part of the way in the horse-drawn omnibus, she found herself looking at the passengers and wondering what they would say if she told them that sentence of death had just been passed upon her.

After Sir John had spoken she had stared at him with wide eyes, shocked to the point when her voice seemed strangled in her throat.

"I am sorry to have to tell you this," Sir John said, "but I can assure you that I am absolutely certain of my facts. You have a heart complaint which is very rare, but it is in fact a disease I have been studying for many years."

He cleared his throat and went on:

"Every Doctor who suspects it sends his patients to me for a final diagnosis, so I cannot suggest that you have a second opinion."

"Is it . . . painful?" Larina managed to gasp.

"In most cases there is no pain whatsoever," Sir John said reassuringly. "I will not burden you with the medical details, but what happens in fact is that your heart suddenly ceases to beat. It may happen when you are asleep, it may occur when you are walking, sitting, even dancing."

"And . . . there is no . . . cure?" Larina asked in a shocked tone.

"None that is known at the moment to the medical profession," Sir John replied. "What I can tell you, as an authority, is that it happens instantly, and when it is diagnosed the patient usually has exactly twenty-one days before the end comes."

"Twenty-one days!" Larina echoed faintly.

As she walked through Sloane Square towards Eaton Terrace she felt that her foot-

22

steps echoed the number on the pavement. Twenty-one! Twenty-one! Twenty-one!

That meant, she told herself, that she would die on the 15th April.

It was a time of year, she thought inconsequentially, she had always loved. The daffodils would be out, there would be blossom on the trees, the chestnuts would be coming into bloom and the sunshine would be particularly welcome because one had missed it during the winter.

On the 16th April she would no longer be here to enjoy it!

She took her key out of her hand-bag and opened the door of number 68 Eaton Terrace.

As she let herself into the narrow Hall, off which opened a small Dining-Room with a tiny Study behind it, she was conscious of the silence and the loneliness of the empty house.

If only her mother were in the Drawing-Room she could run to her to tell her what had happened!

Her mother would have put out her arms and held her close.

But there was no-one to help her now and taking off her hat, Larina walked slowly up the stairs.

Some detached part of her mind noted

that the stair-carpet was very worn: it must have been given hard wear while they were away in Switzerland. Then almost sharply she told herself it was of no consequence.

In twenty-one days she would not be in the house to notice that the carpet was threadbare, that the curtains had faded in the Drawing-Room or the brass bedstead in her room had lost a knob.

Twenty-one days!

She went up another flight of stairs to her bed-room.

There were only two bed-rooms in the house, unless one counted a dark airless place in the basement which had been intended for a maid they could not afford.

Her mother had occupied the front room on the second floor and she had a small slip of a room behind it.

She went into it now and looked round her. All her possessions were here, all the small treasures she had accumulated since childhood.

There was even a Teddy Bear she had loved and taken to bed with her for many years, a doll which opened and shut its eyes, and in the book-case, beside the volumes she had acquired as she grew older, were the first books she had ever owned.

"Not much to show for a life-time!"

Larina told herself.

Then as if the horror of what she had heard swept over her like a flood-tide, she moved to the window to stand looking out over the grey roofs and the back-yards of the houses behind them.

"What can I do? What can I do about it?" Larina asked herself.

Then almost as if the thought came like a life-line to a drowning man she remembered Elvin.

She wondered as she thought of him why he had not come into her thoughts from the very moment Sir John had pronounced the death sentence.

She supposed it must be because she had been shocked into a kind of numbness which had made it impossible for her to think of anything except the twenty-one days which were left to her.

Elvin would have understood exactly what she was feeling; Elvin in his inimitable manner would have made everything seem different.

They had talked of death the very first time they had met.

It had been a day when Mrs. Milton had been very ill and Larina had known by the expression on Dr. Heinrich's face that he was worried.

"There is nothing you can do," he said to Larina. "Go and sit in the garden, I will call you if she needs you."

Larina had known if she was called it would not be a case of her mother needing her, but because Dr. Heinrich thought she was dying.

She had turned and gone blindly out into the garden of the Sanatorium.

For the first time she did not see the brilliance of the flowers or the beauty of the snow-capped mountains which had never failed to make her heart leap when ever she looked at them.

She moved out of sight of the buildings to a place among the pine-trees where there was a seat that had been specially put there for patients who could not walk far.

It was very quiet. There was only the sound of the cascade pouring down the side of the mountain into the valley below and the buzz of the bees as they sucked the honey from the mountain-plants that grew among the rocks.

It was then, because she thought no-one could see her, that Larina had put her hands over her face and begun to cry.

She must have cried for a long time before she heard a movement beside her, and a man's voice said gently:

"Are you crying for your mother?"

Larina with tears still running down her cheeks had turned to see who was there.

A man seated himself beside her and she saw that it was Elvin Farren, an American she had not spoken to before because he slept in a hut by himself in the gardens of the Sanatorium and never came to the Dining-Room for meals.

"Mama is not dead," Larina said quickly as if in answer to a question he had not put into words, "but I know that Dr. Heinrich thinks she may be dying!"

She drew her handkerchief from her belt as she spoke and wiped the tears from her eyes almost fiercely. She was ashamed of having given way so completely.

"You must go on hoping that she will recover," Elvin Farren said.

Larina did not speak for a moment, then she answered:

"I am frightened, but then I suppose everyone is frightened of death."

"Perhaps for other people," Elvin Farren replied, "but not for one's self."

Larina looked at him and knew that he was very ill. He was extremely thin: there was something almost transparent about his skin and the tell-tale patches of bright colour on his cheek-bones were all too obvious.

"You are not afraid?" she asked.

He smiled at her and it seemed to transform his face.

"No."

"Why not?"

He looked away from her towards the panorama of mountains where the sun shining on the snows remaining after the winter was almost blinding.

After a moment he said:

"Do you want the true answer to your question, or the conventional one?"

"I want the true answer," Larina replied. "I am afraid of death because it must be so lonely."

She was thinking of herself as she added:

"Not only for those who die, but also for those who are left behind."

"For those who die," Elvin Farren said, "it is an adventure, a release of the mind, and that in itself is something exciting to look forward to!"

He glanced at her to see if she was following him. Then he went on:

"Have you never thought what an encumbrance one's body is? If it were not hampering us, keeping our feet on the ground, so to speak, we could fly wherever we wished to go! To other parts of the earth, to the moon or, more especially, to the Fourth Dimension."

"I think . . . I understand what you are . . . saying to me," Larina said hesitatingly.

Her grey eyes were wide in her oval face.

This was not the sort of conversation she had ever had with anyone before.

"And as for being alone while we are on earth," Elvin Farren said, "why that is actually impossible!"

"Why?" she asked.

"Because you are a part of everything that is living," he replied. "Look at these flowers."

He pointed as he spoke to a little bunch of blue gentians on the rocks in front of them.

"They are alive," he said, "as much alive as you and I are. They are living, and what is more, they feel even as we feel."

"How do you know that?" Larina asked.

"I have a friend who has been working on the reactions of plant-life for some years," he replied. "He believes, and I believe with him, that a plant has feelings because it contains, as we do . . . the cosmic force which we call life."

"Explain . . . explain it to me," Larina begged.

She was fascinated by what this stranger was telling her, and she turned towards him feeling in some inexplicable manner that she must get closer to him.

"The Buddhists never pick flowers," Elvin began. "They believe by touching one and loving it they share its life and it becomes a part of themselves."

He smiled as he said:

"In my country, the American Indians when they are in need of energy will go into a wood such as this. With their arms extended they will place their backs to a pine-tree and they replenish themselves with its power."

"I can understand that," Larina said, "and I am sure it is true. I have often thought when I have been walking alone in the woods that the trees were pulsatingly alive and that there was a kind of vibration coming from them."

"So when there is life all around you, how could you ever be alone?"

It had been easy to understand what he was saying to her when they were sitting in the pine-woods and looking at the flowers, Larina thought. But in the confines of her little bed-room in Eaton Terrace she felt that she needed help desperately.

If only she could talk to Elvin, she wished, as they had talked together so often after that first meeting.

Mrs. Milton's health had improved and Dr. Heinrich said she was out of danger for the moment. Larina had gone to find Elvin on the balcony of his isolated chalet because she wanted to share her joy with someone.

He invited her to sit down and she realised that from his balcony there was an even more marvellous view of the valley beneath them and the mountains in the distance.

While at first she had been afraid of imposing herself on him, she had soon learnt that he enjoyed seeing her, and whenever she was not with her mother she found her way to his balcony and they would sit talking in the crisp clear air.

Nearly always they spoke of the mystical things that Elvin believed existed in other dimensions.

"This is a material world," he said. "It is merely a shadow of the next which is non-material and very much more advanced mentally and spiritually."

"But suppose someone like myself is not clever enough to understand it?" Larina asked.

"Then you will have to stay here," he replied, "and go on learning and developing until you can."

He had so much to tell her that Larina had begun to count the hours to when she

31

could be with him.

Yet sometimes when he was too ill to walk even as far as his balcony, she would have to wait impatiently until he was better and she could see him again.

She had known without his having to tell her that he had not long to live.

"I am almost looking forward to dying," he said. "There is so much I want to know, so much I want to find out."

Larina gave a little cry of protest.

"Do not talk like that," she begged.

"Why not?" he enquired.

"Because if you go away I shall have no-one to explain such things to me; and when I come to die I shall be afraid . . . very afraid!"

"I have told you there is no reason."

"That is because you are so sure, so certain of what you will find after you are dead," Larina said. "I am not sure, I only want to believe what you tell me, and while I do believe it while I am with you, when you are not there I lose faith."

He had smiled at her as if she were a child.

"When the time comes for you to die," he said, "which will not be for many, many years, call me and I will come to you."

Larina had looked at him wide-eyed.

"You mean . . . ?" she began.

"Wherever I am, whatever I am doing, if

you want me, if you call for me, I will hear you."

He put his hand over hers.

"We will make a pact, Larina. When I am dying I will call for you, and when you die, you will call for me."

"There is no reason why I should not die before you," Larina replied. "I might fall down a mountain or have a train accident."

"And if that happens," Elvin said gravely, "send for me and I will come to you."

"You promise?"

"I promise!" he answered. "Just as you must come to me."

His fingers tightened for a moment on hers.

"I know of no-one I would rather be with when my spirit takes wings."

There was something in the way he said the words which told Larina it was in fact not only the highest compliment he could pay her, but also, in his own way, an expression of love.

She was very inexperienced where men were concerned, having known so few in her life; but she was woman enough to realise that Elvin's thin face lit up when she appeared and there was a look in his eyes that was unmistakable.

If he had not been so emaciated with the

disease which often made him start coughing so convulsively that each spasm left him breathless and exhausted, he would, Larina thought, have been very handsome.

But the disease was eating his life away and she knew even though he was only twenty-five years of age, there was no hope of his survival.

Sometimes when she thought about Elvin in the darkness of the night she wondered whether, if they had met before he fell ill, they would have fallen in love with each other.

She loved him as he was, but as if he were a brother.

She wanted to be with him, she loved talking to him; but because of the way he was suffering she could not think of him as an attractive man, a man to whom she could give her heart.

Nevertheless when one day Elvin told her he was going back to America, she had felt an almost incalculable sense of loss.

"But why? Why?" she asked.

"I want to see my mother," he said. "She is ill, and as I am the youngest member of the family I perhaps mean more to her than my brothers."

"How many brothers have you?" Larina asked.

"Three," he replied. "They are all very clever, very busy with their careers and their families. We have also a sister who is married. I am my mother's baby, and I know at this moment she needs me and therefore I must go to her."

"Will the journey not be too much for you?" Larina asked.

"Does it matter if it is?" he answered again with one of his beguiling smiles.

"It matters to me!" Larina cried. "Oh, Elvin, I shall miss you so much! It will be horrible here without you!"

She paused and then added:

"I could bear it before you came, although sometimes I was the only healthy person in the whole place. But now that I have been with you I cannot imagine how I will fill the days without seeing you, without talking to you. It will be unutterably lonely."

"I have told you that you are never alone," Elvin replied. "When you sit in the garden or on the seat in the pine-woods where we first met, imagine I am there, because in fact I shall be. I shall be thinking of you, and all of me that matters will come to you from America or whatever part of this world or the next I may be in at that particular moment."

"Do you really believe you can get in touch with people by thought?" Larina asked.

"I am completely and utterly convinced of it," Elvin replied. "Thought is stronger than anything else. Thought moves quicker and far more efficiently than anything man can devise, and thought can bring us anything we want — if we want it enough."

"I will think of you," Larina promised.

"Believe that I am near you," Elvin told her, "and I will be!"

Nevertheless once he had gone and the châlet where they had sat together was empty, it was not the same.

Obediently Larina had sat in the garden thinking of him, or had walked, sometimes twice a day, to the seat near the pine-trees.

Then two weeks after he had left her mother became really ill and Larina could think of nothing but her.

Her grief, the tears she shed every night when she was alone, the long journey home alone, the empty house to which she had returned, made it difficult to talk to Elvin in her thoughts, as she had meant to do.

And yet his letters were a source of joy so that she watched for the post and was quite unreasonably disappointed when she did not hear from him.

He had written his first letter to her before he left the Sanatorium and she had received it after he had gone.

It was not a long letter because writing tired him, and she knew he was summoning all his strength for the journey.

He thanked her for all she had meant to him, for the happiness they had shared together, and he finished with the words:

'Never forget that I shall be thinking of you, Larina, that I am near you and if you want me you have only to call and I shall be at your side. Perhaps I shall come back to the Sanatorium when my mother no longer needs me and then we can be together again. You have meant more than I can ever say. God bless you and keep you.'

The next letter was only a few scribbled lines written in the train. Then there had been several after he had reached New York.

He told her that his mother was thrilled to see him and that he was glad that he could be with her because she needed him so badly.

Elvin's letters gave Larina courage even while every day that she was alone in London made her feel more helpless and more lonely.

It had taken her some time to clean up the house after the tenants had left it. She had found it both dirty and untidy.

She was glad in a way that her mother could not see how badly they had treated the things she treasured, how shabby the curtains, carpets and cushions had become in a year.

Larina began to think that one way she could help keep herself would be to take a lodger. It would be easy to rent to someone her mother's bed-room and perhaps the Drawing-Room.

She even began to consider whether two lodgers would not be feasible, if she slept in the Study behind the Dining-Room.

Every time she wrote a cheque for the rent or for her food, she realised how very little there was left in the Bank until she knew she could no longer procrastinate and that it was absolutely essential that she should do something practical about her future.

Sir John had charged her two guineas and she thought as she put the gold sovereigns on his desk that it was a big price to pay for what he had to tell her.

But now that she had reached home she thought that in one way her troubles were over. There would be no need now to find employment, no need to let the rooms, no need to accept strange lodgers.

What was left in the Bank would provide her with enough food for the twenty-one days that remained of her life.

Even to think of it made a quiver of fear run through her.

'Elvin would despise me for being afraid,' she thought, 'but I am, I know I am! I do not want to die! I do not want to find out about the unknown! I want to stay here on earth!'

Suddenly she picked up her hat from where she had laid it down and put it back on her head.

She knew what she was going to do. She was going to tell Elvin what had happened. She was going to send him a cable. It would be expensive, but did money matter at the moment?

Only Elvin would understand — only Elvin could comfort her.

She turned from the mirror and as she did so a sudden thought came to her.

Elvin had said that if she called for him he would come to her.

She would ask him to come, and she was quite sure that he would keep his promise.

Larina ran down the stairs. There was a light in her eyes that had not been there before.

"I will ask Elvin to come to me," she said aloud.

Slamming the front door behind her she began to run down the street towards the Post Office in Sloane Square.

Chapter Two

The funeral cortège drew up outside the brown stone building in Fifth Avenue.

The first carriage contained the three Vanderfeld brothers.

The horses wore black crêpe on their head bands and the coachman a wide crêpe band around his tall hat.

The three Vanderfeld brothers led by the oldest, Harvey, started climbing the long flight of steps to the front door.

On every third step a footman in knee breeches and with powdered hair stood shivering in the pouring rain, a black armband on his crimson livery coat.

Harvey Vanderfeld walked into the large marble Hall where the chandeliers were made of Venetian glass, the Gobelin tapestries came from France, the heavily carved gilt chairs from Italy, and the rugs from Persia.

He walked in his quick characteristic way, passing the waiting flunkeys into the great Drawing-Room, where more footmen were waiting to serve drinks. The Company were to assemble there before they proceeded to luncheon served on gold plates, in the

Mediaeval Dining-Room.

The Drawing-Room was furnished with Louis XIV cabinets, Italian and Dutch pictures and Aubusson carpets. The walls were white, picked out in gleaming gold and the Genoese velvet curtains were decorated with a profusion of tassels and silk fringes.

"Champagne or Bourbon, Mr. Harvey?" the Butler asked.

"Bourbon!" Harvey Vanderfeld replied and immediately lifted a glass to his lips.

His relatives started to file into the room, the women in gowns heavily embellished with crêpe: black veils which they had now pushed back from their faces fell over their shoulders and down their backs.

"It was a beautiful funeral!" a middle-aged woman gushed at Harvey Vanderfeld.

"I am glad you thought so, Cousin Alice."

"And your address, it was magnificent! You were more eloquent than I have ever heard you. There was not a dry eye in the Chapel of the Crematorium."

Harvey Vanderfeld preened himself a little. Then as more relatives of every age came pouring through the double mahogany doors, he said to his brother Gary who was standing beside him:

"I want to speak to you. Come into the Study."

They left the Drawing-Room and walked past several other large Salons to the Study where the walls were covered with leather-bound books which no-one opened. There was large, rather consciously masculine leather furniture and the pictures of horses were by Stubbs.

The brothers had left the Drawing-Room each with a glass of Bourbon in his hand, and finishing his, Harvey Vanderfeld walked to a side-table in the corner of the room to replenish his glass from a decanter.

"It went off well, Gary!" he said.

"Very well, Harvey. I have never heard you speak better!"

"I hope the Press got it all down."

"I am sure they did, and anyway there were copies at the door for those who wanted them."

"Good! I thought the Stars and Stripes draped over the coffin was a pleasant touch, and Mama's long cross of lilies was most touching!"

"You must tell her so," Gary suggested.

"I am quite sure that Wynstan has gone upstairs to do that. I am sorry she could not have been present."

"It would have been too much of an ordeal for her even though she is better."

"I am aware of that, but there is always

something especially poignant in a mother's grief."

"I think the whole country will be grieving with you tomorrow, Harvey, when they read the newspapers."

"If Elvin had to die it could not have been at a better moment than now," Harvey Vanderfeld said, "on the eve of an election when a great number of people have no wish to see Theodore Roosevelt elected for a second term in the White House."

"There are however a large number who admire the strong hand he is taking over the disorders in the Caribbean countries. His policy of extending American power is popular."

"Yankee Imperialism!" Harvey sneered. "If I am elected as President I shall stop all that nonsense! What we should do is look after ourselves at home, not poke our noses into foreign countries which are of no importance to us."

"No need to canvass me, Harvey," Gary replied with a smile. "I have heard you too often on a platform."

"Yes, yes, of course," Harvey agreed.

He was outstandingly handsome but he was thickening about his body and walked like a man older than his thirty-six years. He had however a smile which proved an invaluable vote-catcher.

Gary at thirty-three had already begun to grow fat with too much luxurious living. He also however, had a charm which was inescapable and which was so characteristic of all the Vanderfeld brothers that they had been nick-named by the press, 'The Princes Charming'.

Harvey was the most ambitious and most ruthless. He had fought his way to power, and his stupendous fortune was at the moment being utilised in the most extravagant and most expensive election campaign the United States had ever seen.

He was completely confident that he would beat Theodore Roosevelt and the whole Vanderfeld clan had rallied behind him, eager to find themselves in the White House.

The Vanderfelds were of Dutch origin, and the first member of the family had come to America in the 17th century to live in New Amsterdam, as New York City was then known.

In the following centuries the family fortune was founded to increase with every succeeding generation until the 'House of Vanderfeld' was looked on in America almost as if it were Royalty.

The huge mansion on Fifth Avenue was

only one of their properties. They had a house at Hyde Park on the Hudson River, Gary had recently built himself a marble palace at Newport, and there were ranches, plantations and Estates scattered all over America.

Their mother, Mrs. Chigwell Vanderfeld, had lived in the house on Fifth Avenue ever since she had been widowed, and Harvey's wife, a quiet, unassuming woman, had not attempted to take her place.

It was Mrs. Vanderfeld who decided what should or should not be done by her children, and who was undoubtedly responsible for the good looks of her family as well as their ambition.

She had been a Hamilton and her ancestors had come out from England, but not, as the Vanderfelds always said scornfully, in the overcrowded 'Mayflower' which must have been as large as Noah's Ark.

The ship which had brought their great-great-grandfather from his native Scotland was his own, and he had filled it with a crowd of retainers, their families and their children, so that there was no room for anyone else.

Mrs. Vanderfeld was proud of her Scottish descent, but even more proud of the fact that she came from Virginia, and had been brought up in the middle of the peach country among the foothills of the Blue Ridge Mountains.

Like the Vanderfelds, the Hamiltons had made a fortune, but then they had been only too willing to give up their railway contracting and gold-mining so as to have time to spend their money.

Mrs. Vanderfeld's father had never worked. All his life he enjoyed the life of a country gentleman, administrating his Estate, which was centred round a large roomy house, its pillars, porch, marble Hall and curling staircase an adaptation of English Georgian.

When his daughter said she wished to marry Chigwell Vanderfeld he had not been over-pleased. He had hoped that she would find a husband among what had been left by the Civil War of the gentlemen of Virginia.

He had however little say in the matter. Sally Hamilton was far too self-willed and head-strong to listen to any opposition where her heart was concerned, and she had in fact been extremely happy with her multi-millionaire husband who never stopped working.

Money however was not what she required for her sons: she wanted power, and she made up her mind with a cast-iron determination that Harvey would be the next President of the United States.

It was a determination with which he readily concurred.

"As I have just said," he remarked to his brother, "this funeral could not have come at a better time. Elvin was of course practically unknown to the public or the Press, but I think now he will be fixed in their memory as someone very exceptional, a brother of whom any man could be proud."

Gary did not reply. He had already heard Harvey say almost the identical words in the carriage when they had left the cemetery.

He walked across the room to pour himself another drink, and as he did so the door opened and the Butler came in carrying a silver salver.

"A cable has just come addressed to Mr. Elvin," he said. "I thought, Mr. Harvey, I should bring it to you. It might upset Mrs. Vanderfeld if she saw it."

"Of course," Harvey replied. "Do not take her anything that might be distressing. I have already told one of the secretaries to collect the names of everyone who sent wreaths. I will deal with the letters to express our appreciation. It would be too much for Mrs. Vanderfeld."

"Much too much, Mr. Harvey!" the Butler agreed.

He held out the salver as he spoke and Harvey picked up the cable which lay on it.

He looked at it for a moment, then remarked:

"Mr. Elvin Farren?"

"That was the name Elvin used when he was abroad," Gary explained from the side of the room. "You know we decided that he should not use the family name, since you did not wish the Press to know that he was in a Sanatorium."

"Yes, yes, of course I remember now," Harvey said. "And they never did discover where he was."

"He was of no particular interest to them until he died," Gary said.

There was no sarcasm in his voice. Gary was far too easy-going and good-humoured to be sarcastic.

Harvey opened the cable as the Butler went from the room.

"I see this comes from England," he remarked. "I thought Elvin had been in Switzerland."

"He was," Gary replied.

There was silence then suddenly Harvey ejaculated:

"My God! This cannot be true! There

49

must be some mistake!"

"What is the matter?" Gary asked.

"Listen to this," Harvey said in a sharp voice and read aloud:

"It has happened to me — Stop — I am frightened — Stop — Please keep your promise and come to me — Stop — Your letters my only comfort.

Larina."

Harvey's voice ceased and he stood staring at the paper as if he doubted the sight of his own eyes.

Gary reached his side and looked down at the cable.

"What does it mean?" he asked.

"What does it mean?" Harvey shouted. "Are you crazy? Can't you understand what I have just read out to you? It is perfectly clear to me!"

"What is?" Gary asked.

Harvey walked across the room in an agitated manner as if he could not keep still.

"That this should happen at this moment! Just now! It would have been bad enough at any time, but on the eve of the election — !"

"I do not know what you are talking about," Gary said. "Who is this woman? I have never heard of her."

"Does it matter whether we have heard of her or not?" Harvey asked. "She has heard of Elvin all right, and I suspect she has heard of me too. It is blackmail, dear boy! Blackmail — and we will have to pay it!"

"For what?" Gary asked.

"For her silence — for those letters. Do not be half-witted, Gary! It is obvious that Elvin has put her in the family way and she is having a baby."

"Elvin?" Gary exclaimed. "He has been ill — desperately ill — for years!"

"With consumption, Gary! We all know what consumptives are like sexually, although I did not think it of Elvin."

He put up both his arms towards the ceiling and cried:

"How could he have done this to me at this moment?"

Gary bent to the floor to pick up the envelope in which the cable had arrived.

After a moment he said a little tentatively:

"Whatever Elvin may or may not have done, it appears to me that she does not know who he is. Otherwise why should she address him as Farren rather than Vanderfeld?"

Harvey was still for a moment.

"There is some point in that," he said slowly. "If she does not know, there is hope!"

51

He appeared suddenly to make up his mind and walked across the room to tug at the bell-pull.

The door opened almost instantly.

"Yes, Mr. Harvey?" the Butler enquired.

"Ask Mr. Wynstan to come here immediately!" Harvey said. "If he is not in the Drawing-Room he will be with Mrs. Vanderfeld."

"I'll tell him you want him, Mr. Harvey," the Butler replied in his grave voice.

He closed the door and Harvey once again walked agitatedly across the thick carpet towards the Regency desk and back again.

"I cannot believe it!" he said. "I cannot credit my brother, my own brother, could treat me in such a manner!"

"Elvin cannot have intended to involve you personally in this," Gary said, with just a hint of a smile on his lips.

"But I am involved!" Harvey replied. "You know that as well as I do! Can you imagine what the papers will make of it? It will be a front-page scandal, and how the Republicans will love it! I can just imagine Theodore Roosevelt enjoying every word and making full use of it in his campaign."

"There must be something we can do," Gary said feebly.

As if it might give him inspiration he finished off his drink in one gulp and went to
the side-table to pour himself another.

The two brothers were silent until a few
moments later the door opened and
Wynstan Vanderfeld came in.

At twenty-eight Wynstan was so good-
looking that, as his sister Tracy had told him
often enough, it was 'unfair on women'!

Tall, broad-shouldered and with square-
cut features, he was the Cosmopolitan of
the family and had spent in the last seven
years of his life more time abroad than he
had in America.

"Wynstan," someone once said, "is tradi-
tionally American, overlaid with English
and under-sprung with French!"

But Tracy had summed it up more aptly
when she said:

"Wynstan is the entire creation of Mama
without any help from Papa!"

He certainly was unlike his brothers,
Harvey and Gary, in that his body was slim
and he had the look of an athlete.

He was in fact an outstanding Polo player,
had won many horse races, and at College
had made his name on the baseball field.

As he came into the room now it was no-
ticeable that he had a twinkle in his eye as if
his brothers, like all his other relatives,

amused him and he found it difficult to take them seriously.

"Hudson tells me you need me urgently," he said. "What has happened?"

In answer Harvey held out the cable. Wynstan took it from him and noticed in surprise that his brother's hand was trembling.

He read it carefully and then the twinkle in his eye was even more pronounced as he said:

"If it means what I think it means — good for Elvin! I am glad he had a little fun before he died."

Harvey let out a sound that was like the roar of a lion.

"Is that all you have to say?" he stormed. "Do you not understand what this will mean to me? This is dynamite, Wynstan! Dynamite to my cause and to the election!"

His voice seemed to ring round the room as he continued:

"You know as well as I do that my whole campaign is based on the cries: 'Clean up America!' 'Keep out of Foreign Affairs!' 'Strengthen and support family life which is the foundation of our great Nation!' "

Carried away Harvey declaimed the words and Wynstan gave a little laugh.

"Stop tub-thumping, Harvey!" he said. "Let us talk sensibly!"

"That is just what I am trying to do," Harvey replied.

"It does not sound to me as if this girl, whoever she may be, is trying to threaten your position. She addresses herself to Elvin and pleads with him to come to her."

"Well, he cannot do that!" Harvey snapped. "And what do you think she wants from him except money?"

Wynstan looked at the telegram again.

"Perhaps you have missed that sentence about the letters," Harvey suggested. " 'My only comfort your letters.' What does that mean except that she damned-well thinks she can put a big price on them!"

"It is possible that that is what she intended," Wynstan admitted. "At the same time she says: 'Please keep your promise'. Now what promise could Elvin have made to her?"

"I suppose that he would marry her if she had a child," Gary interposed.

"He cannot do that either!" Harvey said harshly.

"That is true!" Wynstan agreed. "But if she is having Elvin's child, she may have some claim on his Estate."

"My God!" Harvey ejaculated. "I had not thought of that! Do you know what Elvin is worth?"

"I have a vague idea," Wynstan replied. "Father left his fortune, which we all know was considerable, divided between the four of us, after Tracy had been provided for."

"The money does not really matter," Harvey said quickly with an effort. "What is absolutely essential is that there should be no scandal, such as would be inevitable if Elvin's illegitimate child pops up from no-where and asks to be taken into the bosom of the family!"

"I can see the complications," Wynstan said quietly.

"Well, if you can see that, do something about it!" Harvey shouted.

Wynstan looked at him in surprise.

"Why me?"

"Because this blasted woman is English and you are always messing about in that country. You ought to know how to keep her quiet."

Harvey stopped speaking and gave an exclamation.

"That's it! That's it exactly!" he said. "You must keep her quiet at any rate until the election is over. Then we can fight her every inch of the way."

"A very noble sentiment," Wynstan remarked.

"Now don't come the gentleman over

56

me!" Harvey said angrily. "This is a situation where we have to take off our kid-gloves to fight a blackmailer."

"Who said she was a blackmailer?" Wynstan enquired.

"I say she is one, and that is what she damned-well is!" Harvey answered.

"I did point out," Gary said, "that she addresses the cable to Mr. Farren. If she had known Elvin's real name, do you not think she would have used it?"

"That is a very good point, Gary," Wynstan said.

"It does not matter what she calls him," Harvey said impatiently. "If she is having Elvin's child, or pretends she is — for personally I do not believe he was capable of producing one — then she will fleece us down to the last cent. You can be certain of that!"

"I think you have overlooked one thing," Wynstan said in a quiet voice.

"What?" his brother asked.

"Knowing Elvin as I did, and perhaps I knew him better than either of you, I do not believe he would have been interested in the type of woman you are describing."

There was silence for a moment then Harvey said:

"That's all very well. We know what

women are like when they get their hands on a rich man. Elvin was a child in many ways. Against a woman who had deliberately set out to get him he would not have stood a chance."

"Perhaps you are right," Wynstan said reluctantly. "What do you want me to do?"

"I want you to go over to England just as quickly as you can and shut this woman's mouth!" Harvey said. "Strangle her, suffocate her, kidnap her and keep her silent until the election is over. Do anything as long as she does not go near a newspaper reporter or realise how much she can damage me."

Wynstan looked amused as he turned round to put his hand out towards the bell-pull.

"What are you doing? Who are you ringing for?" Harvey enquired.

"I have to find out something about Larina or whatever her name is," he said. "She has signed only her Christian name, and there is no address."

"No-one must know about this," Harvey said quickly. "If the newshawks get even a smell of it, I am finished!"

"I am going to speak to Prudence," Wynstan said soothingly as if speaking to a child. "Prudence has been with Elvin ever since he came back from Europe, she has also been with us since before I was born. I imagine we can trust her after all these years."

"Yes, of course," Harvey agreed in a somewhat shamefaced manner.

The Butler opened the door.

"Ask Prudence to come downstairs for a moment, Hudson," Wynstan said to him. "I imagine she is back by now from the funeral."

"Yes, Mr. Wynstan, she is upstairs."

"We would like to speak to her."

"Of course, Mr. Wynstan."

The door closed and Wynstan stood in front of the fireplace.

"Stop being so agitated, Harvey!" he said after a moment. "You are sweating, and anyone who knew you would know that you are frightened!"

"I am frightened!" Harvey said. "I do not mind telling you, Wynstan, this is a stab in the back which I had not anticipated, and certainly not from one of my own brothers!"

"I think you are being unnecessarily apprehensive," Wynstan said, "but because I am fond of you, Harvey, and Elvin meant a great deal to me, I will certainly try and see if I can solve this problem."

"Pay anything — anything," Harvey said,

"but keep her quiet, that is all I ask. Keep her quiet!"

When Prudence came into the room she looked surprised to see all three brothers together in the Study while, as she knew, the big Drawing-Room was filled with their relatives and friends.

She was an elderly woman with a kind, open face which made adults and children alike trust her instinctively. Her eyes were red and a little swollen from weeping.

She was dressed, as she always had been ever since the brothers could remember, in a dress of grey cotton with stiff white collar and cuffs that were always spotlessly clean.

She had grown stouter and heavier over the years, Wynstan thought as she walked towards them, but otherwise she had changed very little from when as a child he had said his first prayers at her knee and she had taught him his alphabet.

"Come in, Prudence," he said. "We want your help, which is nothing unusual!"

"What's happened?" Prudence asked looking from Wynstan to Harvey and then at Gary.

"We want you to tell us what you know about a woman called Larina," Wynstan replied.

Prudence did not hesitate.

"She was a friend of Mr. Elvin's."

"What sort of friend?" Harvey questioned quickly.

"I think it was someone he met while he was in Switzerland," Prudence answered. "He had several letters from her after he returned and I know that he wrote to her."

"Where are they? Where are the letters?" Harvey asked. "Fetch them at once."

"I can't do that, Mr. Harvey," Prudence said.

"Why not?"

"Because Mr. Elvin burnt them."

"Burnt them?" Harvey exclaimed.

"Yes, a few days before he died he said to me: 'Prudence, I think I had better tidy up my possessions. Bring me my special box.' "

"What box was that?"

Prudence looked at Wynstan.

"You remember it, Mr. Wynstan."

"Yes, I gave it to him," Wynstan said. "He must have been fifteen at the time. I remember saying that every man should have a place where he could lock away papers he did not want everyone else to read."

Wynstan paused and smiled as he added:

"That was after I found Mama reading letters I had received from a girl-friend of whom she did not approve."

"She must have been kept busy if she read

all your love letters!" Gary teased.

"Go on, Prudence," Wynstan said quietly.

"I fetched the box to his bed and he took out some poems he had been writing from time to time. Sometimes he would read them to me and sometimes he would not. He looked at them and said:

" 'Burn these, Prudence!'

" 'Why?' I asked. 'They're beautiful, Mr. Elvin! Let's keep them. Someone might publish them one day.'

" 'That is what I am afraid of and it would not be because they wanted to understand what I was trying to say,' he answered. 'Burn them, Prudence!' "

Prudence made a little gesture with her hands.

"So I burnt them."

"And what else?" Wynstan asked.

"The letters he had kept over the years, one or two from you, Mr. Wynstan, some from his mother, and those he had received from the young lady."

"How do you know they were from her?" Wynstan asked.

"They were the only letters he received after he returned home," Prudence answered, "and he seemed happy to have them. He also said to me: 'Don't you think

Larina is a pretty name, Prudence? I think it is lovely!' "

Harvey's eyes met his brother Gary's.

"What was her surname, Prudence?" he asked.

"I don't know, Mr. Harvey!"

"But you must have some idea."

"No, Mr. Elvin never told me anything about her."

There was silence, then as if she knew the brothers were perturbed, Prudence said:

"But Mr. Renour will know it."

"Renour? Why should he know it?" Harvey asked in surprise.

"Because Mr. Elvin wrote to her and it would be entered in the post-book."

"Of course!" Wynstan exclaimed. "I had forgotten that we kept a post-book in the house! He will also have her address."

"Of course," Prudence agreed.

"Then would you be kind enough to ask him to bring the post-book here to us?" Wynstan said. "And thank you, Prudence, for your help."

"I hope I have been able to assist you," Prudence said looking from one to the other.

She waited for a second then she said:

"Thank you, Mr. Harvey, for the beautiful things you said at the Service. I'm sure

Mr. Elvin would have been pleased."

Tears came into her eyes as she spoke and she turned quickly and went from the room.

"Beautiful things!" Harvey said scornfully. "I wonder what Prudence would say if she knew the truth."

"You certainly made Elvin a cross between the Archangel Gabriel and St. Sebastian," Wynstan remarked.

"All the more reason why he should not get knocked off his pedestal!" Harvey snapped.

"Now stop agitating yourself!" Gary pleaded. "Wynstan said he will help and he is pretty efficient when he makes up his mind to do something."

"Thank you!" Wynstan said with an amused smile.

The door opened and Hudson came in.

"Prudence said you wanted the postbook, Mr. Harvey," he said, "but Mr. Renour is not yet back from the funeral so I have brought it myself."

"Thank you very much, Hudson."

Harvey took it from him and turned the pages quickly.

"I had no idea we sent out so many letters from this house!" he remarked. "With what we contribute the Post Office should pay a dividend!"

Neither of his brothers answered and he

knew they were waiting impatiently to see what he would find.

"Here it is!" he said at length. "Miss Larina Milton, 68 Eaton Terrace, London, England."

"Well, at least we know where she is!" Gary said.

"I suppose you want me to see her as soon as possible?" Wynstan said in a resigned voice. "I will do it, but I would like to point out that it is extremely inconvenient. I have a new car being delivered tomorrow and there are two polo ponies I wish to train before the games start in May."

"Polo ponies!" Harvey said with a groan which was also a sound of contempt.

"I have an idea!" Gary said suddenly.

Both brothers turned to look at him.

"What is it?" Wynstan enquired.

"I have just thought that the election will be reported in the English newspapers. Even if this girl had no idea who Elvin was when he was in Switzerland, she will read about Harvey and they may easily mention Elvin's death. Then she will know —"

"Just how much money she can get out of us!" Harvey interjected. "She would up her price every day of the campaign."

Wynstan did not speak and Harvey went on:

"Gary is right — of course he is right! It is no use your seeing her in London and trying to keep her quiet. You have got to get her away. Take her to France — Spain — Italy — anywhere so long as the newspapers are not delivered regularly every morning."

"We have no reason to suppose that she already knows that Elvin was a Vanderfeld," Wynstan said.

"We have no reason to be sure she does not!" Harvey retorted. "It would be a mistake to take a risk. Besides although Elvin became pathetically thin after he got so ill, there is a likeness about us all. Mama has often remarked on it."

"And added that Wynstan is much the best-looking!" Gary said.

"Do not let it make you jealous!" Wynstan remarked. "It is often a liability!"

"You can hardly expect us to believe that!" Gary laughed. "You know as well as I do, Wynstan, that the girls fall down like a set of ninepins whenever you appear."

"I tell you it is often a liability!" Wynstan insisted.

"Oh, keep to the point!" Harvey said irritably. "Gary has had a good idea. We must consider it. Where can you take her, Wynstan?"

"Presuming of course that she will go with

me," Wynstan replied. "I presume also that you want me to tell her that Elvin is dead?"

"No, I have a better idea," Harvey said.

"What is it?"

"In this cable she has sent to Elvin she has begged him to come to her, and it is obvious that he promised her he would. Well then, he must keep his promise."

"What do you mean by that?" Wynstan asked.

Harvey's eyes narrowed a little, as those who did business with him on Wall Street knew always happened when he was doing a big deal.

"We will send her a cable from Elvin saying that he will meet her at the Villa. That ought to get her away from London."

"The Villa in Sorrento?" Wynstan asked. "Good Lord, I have not been there for years!"

"Grace and I spent a fortnight there in 1900," Gary said. "It is being kept up in just the same way as when grandfather built it, or rather restored it to its Roman glory, and spent a fortune in the process!"

"As a matter of fact I would rather like to see it again," Wynstan said. "I remember as a child thinking it was the most beautiful place in the world."

"Then that is settled," Harvey said briskly

determined to get back to business. "We will send her a telegram and sign it with Elvin's name."

"You had better take it to the Post Office yourself. It cannot be sent from here. Renour must not know about this."

"Supposing she refuses to go?" Gary said. "Besides, you cannot expect a woman to travel all that way alone."

"No, of course not," Harvey said impatiently. "Why do we keep that large, expensive office in London except to do what they are told in a situation like this?"

His lips tightened, then he went on:

"On second thoughts, we will cable Donaldson to see this woman and persuade her to go to Italy."

He paused to explain:

"No point in her receiving anything else signed by Elvin — it might strengthen her case against us."

"I can see that," Gary remarked.

"Then we tell Donaldson," Harvey went on, "to arrange for the Villa to be got ready for Wynstan, and to get Larina, or whatever her name is, there as soon as possible. If he cannot take her himself, he can send a competent Courier with her. It is only a question of organization."

Harvey paused to look at his brothers

for their approval.

"It is certainly an idea," Wynstan said slowly.

"Have you a better one?"

"No, and I would much prefer to argue this thing out in Sorrento rather than in London."

"I am glad somebody is pleased about it!" Harvey said in an exasperated voice. "I shall not have a moment's peace or a good night's sleep until I know you have settled this matter, Wynstan. I am relying on you to save the people who have given me their faith and trust."

There was almost a sob in his voice.

His brother laughed.

"Spare me the dramatics, Harvey! I will do my best, although I do not mind telling you I find it an intolerable nuisance to have to go traipsing off to Europe just when I want to be at home."

A sudden thought struck him.

"What are we going to tell Mama?"

"Oh, God!" Harvey ejaculated, then quickly he added:

"We will just have to pretend that you have had an urgent message from one of your lady-friends."

"She is not going to be pleased about that!" Wynstan said. "And she particularly wants me here now when she is so upset about Elvin."

"Mama will always accept that affairs of the heart — yours at any rate — come first!" Harvey said with an almost spiteful note in his voice.

"And I think," Gary interrupted, "she is secretly rather proud of your success. She thinks you are a chip off the old Hamilton block, who from what Mama tells us behaved in a very reprehensible manner with the lassies in the heather before they were told to get out of Scotland!"

"I will think of something to tell her," Wynstan said in a weary voice, "but if I find that you, Harvey, have been decrying me behind my back or saying any unpleasant things such as you have said in the past, I swear I will tell her the truth."

"I promise you I will support you in every possible way," Harvey replied. "And another reason why it is so important for you not to go to London is that Tracy might ask questions. We do not want that supercilious Duke of hers looking down his aristocratic nose and saying that the English do not get into this sort of jam!"

"Personally, I like Osmund," Wynstan said. "He is not supercilious to me. At the same time it is important that Tracy should not learn about this, if indeed there is any-thing to learn."

He walked towards the door.

"Personally, I think I shall find that the whole drama is a figment of Harvey's fertile imagination."

"Where are you going?" Harvey asked hastily. "We have to compile a cablegram."

"You can do that without me," Wynstan answered. "If I have to sail across the Atlantic, which let me say is the last thing I want to do at this moment, I might as well do it in comfort. The *'Kaiser Wilhelm der Grosse'* sails tomorrow morning, and I will be on her."

He left the room and closed the door behind him.

Gary and Harvey looked at each other.

"I congratulate you, Harvey," Gary said. "I never thought for one moment that Wynstan would agree to what you suggested."

"Frankly neither did I," Harvey replied.

Wynstan boarded the *'Kaiser Wilhelm der Grosse'* just before she was ready to leave New York harbour on the morning tide.

The ship that held the Atlantic Blue Riband carried 28 per cent of all the passengers landed in New York. She was noted as being fitted out with every comfort and also providing the maximum amount of entertainment with which to while away the passage across the ocean.

Wynstan was however more interested in the passenger-list of which he had taken a copy from the Purser's office.

Although his booking had been made at the last moment, the magic name of Vanderfeld had secured for him one of the best suites and only the Purser was aware of how difficult it had been to re-allot the other passengers without causing offence.

However as an experienced traveller, Wynstan approved his cabins, tipped his stewards, which he always did at the beginning of the voyage, and left his valet to arrange things in the manner he found most comfortable.

He settled himself down in an arm-chair, ordered a drink, and studied the passenger-list.

There had been no-one to wave him good-bye on the Quay, a custom he always detested. It suited him that Harvey had been insistent that he should creep out of America as quietly as possible, so that no-one, except his immediate family, should be aware that he was leaving.

"For God's sake, Wynstan, do not get involved with the Press," he said. "You know what they are like if they suspect that anything unusual is occurring."

Wynstan however had been concerned less about the Press than about his mother.

"I thought you would stay with me, darling," Mrs. Vanderfeld said tearfully when he told her he had to sail to Europe immediately.

"I know, Mama, and I wished to be with you now," Wynstan replied, "but I have unfortunately promised to help this friend of mine if he was ever in trouble, and now he is keeping me to my promise."

"He?" Mrs. Vanderfeld asked suspiciously. "You do not expect me to believe, Wynstan, that there is not a woman at the bottom of it?"

"Your mind invariably works in the same direction, Mama," Wynstan replied with a smile. "There must be some French blood in you because your maxim is always *'cherchez la femme'!*"

"With reason!" Mrs. Vanderfeld replied. "I thought you had finished your affair with that French actress, what was her name?"

"Gaby Deslys," Wynstan answered. "How did you know about her?"

"I hear about everything," Mrs. Vanderfeld said with satisfaction, "and although you are determined not to tell me the truth about this hasty journey of yours, you can be sure I will learn every detail about it sooner or later!"

"I am sure you will, Mama," Wynstan agreed.

His mother looked at him as he sat on the end of her enormous bed, an imitation of the elaborate blue and silver one used by King Ludwig of Bavaria.

The curtains, dressing-table cover, pillow cases and the edges of the sheets were all edged with real Venetian lace, and there was a balustrade separating the bed from the rest of the room as in most Royal State bed-rooms in France and Bavaria.

"I suppose," Wynstan had said when he first saw it, "that only princes of the blood are allowed behind the balustrade."

"Really, Wynstan, you are not to say such things!" his mother had replied.

At the same time she loved it when he teased her, especially about her admirers of whom she had quite a number even in her old age.

"You know, Wynstan," she said now looking at his handsome face appreciatively, "I think you are a throwback to one of my forbears who was a pirate and buccaneer at the time of Queen Elizabeth. He had a way with women. Otherwise, the Queen would have had little use for him."

"And yet she remained a virgin," Wynstan said.

"I have often had my doubts about that!" Mrs. Vanderfeld remarked, and her son laughed.

"If you talk like that in front of Harvey, Mama, he will have a stroke! He is running his whole campaign on purity and insists that we must all be Puritans!"

"It is the last thing I have ever wanted to be," Mrs. Vanderfeld said sharply. "Harvey is an old woman — he always has been! At the same time I would like to see him at the White House."

"And so would I," Wynstan said. "It would make him so happy, and at least he is a great deal better-looking than Theodore Roosevelt!"

"That would not be difficult!" Mrs. Vanderfeld snapped, "but I am not certain you would not make a more effective President!"

Wynstan put up his hands in horror.

"Have you forgotten I am the play-boy of the family?"

"Is it not time you began to think about settling down?" Mrs. Vanderfeld asked. "You have had a great deal of fun in the past few years, and I do not blame you. But I would like to see your son before I die."

Wynstan laughed.

"That is a very good line, Mama, but you are not really thinking of dying, although you give us a fright occasionally, as you did last month. You know really you are as tough as your pioneering ancestors and you will easily live to be a hundred!"

"I might do that just to spite you all!" Mrs. Vanderfeld said. "As long as I am alive I can keep the family under control, at least where the others are concerned!"

"And I am the exception?" Wynstan asked.

"You always were an obstinate, uppity little boy," Mrs. Vanderfeld said, "but you managed, even when you were very young, to charm a bird off a tree if it suited you."

"It always suited me where you were concerned, Mama," Wynstan said, "and I think the reason I have never married is that I have never found anyone half as amusing, as witty, or as attractive as you."

"There you go!" Mrs. Vanderfeld exclaimed. "Now I am quite certain that you have something to hide from me, or you would not be going out of your way to flatter me."

She looked at her son and her eyes twinkled rather like his.

"Do what you have to do," she said, "then come back and tell me all about it. I get a vicarious excitement at my age hearing about your love-affairs."

"As a change from your own, Mama?" Wynstan asked and again she laughed.

She had however kissed him very tenderly when he said good-bye to her.

"Take care of yourself, my darling," she said softly. "You are my baby now that Elvin is gone and I shall be thinking about you and praying that you will come back safely."

"I will be back, Mama," Wynstan replied, "and just as quickly as I can manage it."

"And remember what I have said about that son of yours," Mrs. Vanderfeld cried as he reached the door.

"You have enough men loving you already," Wynstan replied and they were both laughing as he shut the door of her bed-room.

Looking down at the list of 332 first class passengers Wynstan found a name that held his attention.

The Earl and Countess of Glencairn were on 'B' deck.

He had known the Earl for some years, an elderly Peer, who had once been an outstanding rider to hounds. He had broken his leg when he was over seventy and now had to spend his time in a wheel-chair.

He had, however, a few years before this happened taken as his second wife an extremely attractive dark-eyed Frenchwoman.

She had had a somewhat chequered career in Paris, and it had undoubtedly been an achievement on her part to confound those who criticized her by stepping into the English Peerage.

Wynstan had met her six months before when she had dined with his sister at the Duke's magnificent house near Oxford. He had sat next to her at dinner, and she had flirted with him in a manner which had told him they were both masters of the ancient art.

There was a slightly cynical smile on Wynstan Vanderfeld's lips as he put down the passenger-list.

The voyage would not be as boring as he had anticipated.

Chapter Three

Larina felt as if her heart had already stopped beating.

She could think of nothing except that the days, hours and minutes were passing and while she felt she ought to do something special, something important before she died, she had no idea how to set about it.

She felt as if her will-power had dissolved and she needed, more than she had ever needed in her life before, someone to take control of the situation and tell her what to do.

She could only wait with a kind of hopelessness for Elvin's reply to her cable.

Supposing, she thought, he was too ill to answer her cry for help?

Because the idea made her frantic she would take out his letters every hour and read the last one she had received from him from America.

He told her how pleased his mother had been to see him and also that he had in fact stood the journey far better than he expected.

"I think the sea air did me good," he

wrote. "It made me think of you and a grey day reminded me of your eyes."

His letters were not long and Larina knew that even if he had wished to write more it would have been too much of an effort.

And yet he had said he felt better. That in itself was encouraging and she was sure that Elvin was alive, otherwise she would have been aware of it.

Because she had felt so terribly lonely when she first returned to London she had tried to remember all he had told her.

"How can you ever be alone," he had said, "when there is life all around you?"

Remembering his words and telling herself how much they must mean to her now that she had no one to turn to in her loneliness, she had walked through the streets into Hyde Park.

It was a relief to get away from the little house which was so silent and oppressive, and there was a sharpness in the wind which made her think of the clear, crisp air of Switzerland.

She walked across the green grass until she reached the Serpentine and although it had been a dull day until then, a pale sun came out and she sat down on a bench near the water.

She looked around and realised that the

daffodils were in bloom and the red tulips stood in the flower-beds like Guardsmen.

She had been so intent on her worries which encompassed her like a fog, that walking through the Park she had seen nothing and been aware of nothing except her fear of the future and the difficulties of getting a job.

She pretended that Elvin was there beside her, telling her that there was life everywhere and that she was a part of it.

"Oh, Elvin, Elvin!" she whispered. "Help me! Help me!"

She felt as if she shouted the words aloud. But there was no reply, only the rustle of the wind blowing the dead leaves which still lay beneath the trees and the movement of the branches overhead which were just beginning to show the first green buds of spring.

She wind rippled the water of the Serpentine and the daffodils bent their heads as the breeze touched them.

"I am a part of it, and it is a part of me," Larina told herself, but she felt they were only words and she could not really understand them.

Then suddenly there was a light on the water that was almost blinding, the daffodils were as golden as the sun itself and she could almost see the grass growing beneath her feet.

It was intense, magic, divine, a glory which lighted the sky and her soul.

She was one with it and it was part of her!

Then as she longed to cling to the vividness and the beauty of it, to hold it close, to be sure it was really happening, it was gone!

It was so momentary, such a transitory experience, that when it was past she thought it must have been an illusion. Yet at the same time she knew it had happened!

"Now I understand what Elvin was saying," she told herself.

She tried to recapture the radiance, but while the sun was still on the water, it had not the light that she had seen for that one incredible moment.

"Perhaps it will grow easier with practice," Larina hoped.

The moment of magic glowed like a jewel in her mind as she walked homewards.

It had uplifted and elated her, but it was not exactly comforting. It just made her long more desperately for Elvin to tell her more, to be with her.

She did not forget it as the days passed; she kept trying to make it happen again; but the ecstasy and the wonder eluded her.

Now she could think of nothing but the

moment when her heart beating in her breast would stop; when the breath moving in and out of her lungs would cease.

She could only call out to Elvin, as he had told her to do, in her mind and pray that he would answer her cable.

Only Elvin could keep her from being terrified as she knew she would be when the twenty-first day arrived.

If Elvin could not leave at once, it would be too late, and even if he did they would only have a very short time together!

It seemed impossible that what she had said to him in Switzerland had come true.

"I might easily die before you," she had told him, but she had not meant it.

It had just been a way of talking, but now she knew she would not outlive Elvin, and she was not prepared, as he was, to face the inevitability of death.

'Help me, help me!' she cried in her heart as she walked home.

She felt there was something almost menacing about the empty house as she entered the door which needed painting, saw the shabby stair-carpet and felt the silence.

Neither she nor her mother had cared much for 68 Eaton Terrace.

They had in fact both hated leaving their big comfortable home in Sussex Gardens on the other side of the Park.

When Dr. Milton had died unexpectedly from a virus he had caught from one of his patients, his wife found the house belonged to his partners in the practice.

Larina and her mother had also discovered in consternation that he had left very little money.

Dr. Milton had a fairly lucrative practice amongst well-to-do people who lived in that part of London.

But being a man of deep compassion and sympathy, he treated a great number of the poor in the slums around Paddington without charging them a fee, and moreover out of his own pocket, he often provided them with medicines and small luxuries they could not afford for themselves.

Many of his poorer patients carrying pathetic little bunches of flowers attended his funeral, all of them ready to talk of the 'good doctor' and his kindness.

At the same time it was depressing to realise how little money he had left his wife and daughter.

Because her mother was so unhappy and in a state of collapse after her father's death it had been left to Larina to find them a place to live.

Because she thought it was a good idea for

her mother's sake to get away from the neighbourhood where she had been so happy, Larina had gone south of the Park and searched round Belgravia for a cheap house to rent.

The one she had found in Eaton Terrace was certainly cheap, but it seemed small, stuffy and unattractive even after it had been furnished with the things they brought with them.

"It is stupid of me, I know," Mrs. Milton had said after they had been in it a few weeks, "but I find it difficult to think of this house as home."

She was finding it, Larina knew, far more difficult to adjust herself to being a widow with no husband to take care of her.

Mrs. Milton had always been cosseted and loved all her life. She had no desire for independence nor was she interested in the much talked of emancipation of women.

"I do not want to vote, darling," she said to her husband once in Larina's hearing. "I am quite content for you to explain the political situation to me if I have to hear about it, and, quite frankly, I would rather talk of something else."

"I am afraid you will never make an efficient modern woman," her husband had replied with a smile.

"I just want to be your wife," Mrs. Milton had said with an adoring look in her eyes.

They had been so happy together that sometimes Larina had felt unwanted.

Yet she knew that her father loved her deeply, and when he died her mother clung to her in a manner which assured her over and over again how much she mattered.

But now she was alone and she realised how unfit she was to endure loneliness after the close companionship she had enjoyed with her parents.

"Perhaps it is a good thing to have so short a time to live," she told herself somewhat bitterly. "I have been brought up in the wrong way to cope with a world where a woman is helpless alone."

She thought of how when she was on her way to visit Sir John Coleridge she had been planning that she must get a job as a secretary.

It had been an idea, but she knew that there was a great deal of unemployment in the country at the moment and it was very unlikely that anyone would employ a woman when they could obtain the services of a man.

Restlessly she walked up to the Drawing-Room to look at her mother's special treasures: the work-box of inlaid marquetry in which she had always kept her embroidery, the little French writing-desk between the windows on which stood photographs of her father and herself.

She touched the china ornaments on the mantelpiece which had been a present one Christmas and which her mother had loved because they were so pretty.

Looking at them Larina noticed that the china shepherdess's hand was missing.

She felt angry that the tenants should have been so careless and had not even repaired the broken piece. Then she asked herself why should it matter?

Her mother would not know that the precious mementoes of her married life had been damaged, and in a few days she herself would not be there to see them either.

"What am I to do with all these things?" Larina asked herself in a sudden fright. "I cannot just die without telling someone I have no further use for them."

She tried to think of a friend in whom she could confide. But while her father and mother had many acquaintances where they had been living in Sussex Gardens, she had, by usual convention, not been allowed to take part in the social entertaining given by her parents.

Being shy, she had not made friends with

the few girls she had met. But her mother had always talked as if everything would alter when she was grown up.

"We must give a Ball for Larina," she had said to her husband once. "You had better start saving, John, because when she is eighteen, I intend to be very extravagant about her clothes, especially her evening-gowns."

"You will be saying next that you want to present her at Court!" Dr. Milton replied.

"Why not?" his wife asked. "I was presented when I was eighteen!"

"Your family lived in rather different circumstances," the Doctor replied.

"All the Courtneys were presented," her mother said with dignity, "and I would not feel I was doing my duty by Larina unless she went to Buckingham Palace to make her curtsey."

She smiled at her daughter as she spoke and said:

"If they do not think I am important enough to present you, my darling, I shall ask your godmother, Lady Sanderson. She has always sent you a present at Christmas. Although she lives in the country and we seldom meet, I know she is still the dear friend she always was."

But Lady Sanderson had died the following year and her mother had wept at losing a friend who had meant a great deal to her, Larina gathered, in her childhood.

So there was no Lady Sanderson to whom she could turn now, and having been away for a year in Switzerland, and the year before that being in deep mourning, she found it was difficult even to remember the names of the people who had come to the house in Sussex Gardens.

"Besides," Larina asked herself, "who wants to meet someone who merely seeks comfort because they are afraid of their approaching death?"

She knew that apart from anything else she would feel shy to talk about the fate which hung over her like the sword of Damocles.

'I will keep it to myself,' she thought with sudden pride. 'I will not whine and complain as women used to do to Papa.'

She could remember her father saying once:

"I am fed up with grizzling women!"

"What do you mean, 'grizzling women'?" her mother asked with a smile.

"The ones who have more aches and pains than anyone else! Needless to say, they are always the richest! The poor are concerned with the fundamentals such as being born, keeping alive and having the bravery to die, as one man said to me, 'with his boots on'."

"They have courage," Mrs. Milton said softly.

"That is what I admire about them," the Doctor said. "Many of them are bad, the reformers call them wicked, but at least they have guts! It is the other sort I cannot stand!"

"I must not complain . . . I must be brave," Larina told herself. "I would want Papa to be proud of me."

She sat down on the sofa and wondered what she should do. There were things that wanted mending and quite a lot of the furniture needed repairing.

But what was the point of doing it?

It was then that there came the sound of the front-door bell ringing in the basement. She could hear it quite clearly in the empty silence of the house.

'Whoever can it be?' she wondered then suddenly thought it might be a cable from Elvin.

She jumped to her feet and there was a light in her eyes that had not been there before as she ran down the stairs.

Hastily she pulled open the front-door, but it was not a telegraph-boy who stood there as she had expected, but a man, middle-aged, well-dressed and wearing a bowler hat.

He appeared to Larina to be a kind of superior clerk or perhaps someone in the Civil Service as a number of her father's patients had been.

"Does Miss Larina Milton live here?" he asked.

"I am Miss Milton!"

She saw there was a faint look of surprise in his eyes as if he had not expected her to open the door.

Then because she felt it might seem strange to admit that she was alone in the house Larina added:

"I am afraid the maid is out!"

"May I speak with you, Miss Milton?" the man asked.

He had removed his bowler hat when she had appeared and she saw his hair was grey and she told herself he looked extremely respectable.

At the same time she did not like to let him into the house.

"What is it about?" she enquired.

As she spoke she wondered if in fact he had come to sell her something.

She was well aware it was often the most unlikely looking people who hawked insurance or expensive goods for sale from door to door.

"I have had a communication from Mr. Elvin Farren," the man replied.

Her suspicions vanished.

"Oh, will you come in?" she asked quickly.

The man did as she asked, wiping his feet carefully on the mat. He was rather large and it was difficult for him to squeeze past her in the narrow Hall, but he managed it and waited while she closed the door.

"Will you come upstairs to the Drawing-Room?" she asked. "It is on the first floor."

He put his hat down on a chair and waited at the bottom of the stairs for her to precede him.

Larina led the way.

As they entered the Drawing-Room, despite the faded curtains and the worn carpet it looked quite attractive in the late afternoon sunshine coming through the narrow windows.

"Will you sit down?" Larina asked politely.

"My name is Donaldson, Miss Milton," the man said as he seated himself on the edge of the sofa while Larina took an arm-chair opposite him.

"You have heard from Mr. Farren?" she asked eagerly.

"Mr. Farren asked me to call on you," Mr. Donaldson said. "I understand, Miss Milton, from what he said in his cable that you wish to see him."

"Yes, I want to see him very much," Larina answered and added, ". . . if it is possible."

"Mr. Farren has suggested that you should meet in Sorrento."

"In Sorrento?" Larina ejaculated. "In Italy?"

"Yes, Miss Milton, his family have a Villa there and Mr. Farren suggested that I arrange for you to go there immediately."

Larina looked at him in astonishment.

"Did he suggest that I should travel . . . all that . . . way to see him?"

"He will be coming a great deal further from America," Mr. Donaldson said, "and I imagine that he thought it would not be too much to ask you to make the journey from here."

"No, no, of course not!" Larina said. "It is not that it is too much to ask, it is just that it was such a surprise!"

"You know where Sorrento is, Miss Milton?"

"Yes, of course," Larina answered. "It is near Naples. My father has often spoken to me of Naples. He was very interested in

Pompeii and Herculaneum."

"They have made some great discoveries there, I believe," Mr. Donaldson said.

"So I have read."

Larina was talking automatically because her brain was dazed with the idea that had been presented to her.

She had naturally supposed that if Elvin was able to keep his promise he would come to London.

He had told her once that when he stayed in London he went to a hotel called Claridges, and Larina had imagined she would be able to visit him in his Sitting-Room there and perhaps he would be well enough to come to her house.

But Sorrento!

She felt as if she could not take it in.

"Mr. Farren was not, of course, expecting you to travel alone," Mr. Donaldson was saying. "He asked that I should either escort you there myself or engage a Courier for you."

Larina did not speak and after a moment he went on:

"Perhaps I should explain, Miss Milton, that I look after Mr. Farren's interests in London where he has an office."

"An office?" Larina asked in surprise. "Why would he need an office?"

There was a pause before Mr. Donaldson answered:

"Mr. Farren has various business interests not only in his own country but also in Europe, which we look after for him."

"Oh, I see," Larina said.

She had thought that Elvin must be fairly rich, otherwise he would not have been able to afford a chalet by himself. She knew also that apart from herself and her mother, Dr. Heinrich's fees were very high.

But an office to look after his business affairs suggested considerable wealth and it did not seem like Elvin somehow to be concerned with material things.

Yet Mr. Donaldson was continuing in a brisk, businesslike way:

"What I am suggesting, Miss Milton, is that you leave everything to me. I'll make your journey as comfortable as possible. All I want to know is how soon you can leave."

"How soon?" Larina questioned in a bewildered manner.

"Mr. Farren seemed to think it was important that you should go to Italy as soon as possible. I am not quite certain how quickly he can be there."

There was a moment's pause and then Larina said:

"H-have you any . . . idea how much it would . . . cost?"

She felt embarrassed as she asked the question.

"I'm afraid I'm explaining myself very clumsily," Mr. Donaldson answered. "If you go to Italy, Miss Milton, it'll be as Mr. Farren's guest. He made that very clear in the cable. I'll see to all the expenses."

"But I do not . . . think I could permit . . ." Larina began, then her voice died away.

What was the point of protesting?

If Elvin wanted her to go to Sorrento the only way it would be possible for her to get there would be at his expense.

She knew quite well that she had not enough money left in the Bank to buy her ticket.

It was ridiculous to make difficulties or to argue about anything when Elvin was being so kind, so overwhelmingly kind in responding to her cry for help.

She had wondered after sending the cable if she could have worded it better. But somehow she thought he would understand what she was trying to say, and it was quite obvious now that he had done so.

He was coming to her aid; he was helping her as he had promised he would; she must agree to anything he suggested.

Mr. Donaldson was watching her from the sofa.

"All you have to tell me, Miss Milton," he said after a moment, "is how soon you can be ready."

Larina looked rather helplessly around the room, then she answered:

"I would be ready at once, if it were not for one thing."

"And what is that, Miss Milton?"

"I shall have to sell the contents of this house," Larina replied. "I need the money . . . I must have some new clothes if I am going to Sorrento."

She felt Mr. Donaldson looked surprised and she explained:

"You see, I have been living in Switzerland, which is where I met Mr. Farren. We wore thick clothing there as it was very high up and even in the summer it could be very cold in the evenings. But Sorrento will be warm."

"It will indeed," Mr. Donaldson agreed. "In fact I should think it will be getting really hot as soon as we move into April."

"That is what I thought," Larina agreed.

"I can quite understand that you need some summer dresses," Mr. Donaldson said.

He smiled and it gave him a humanity

which had been rather lacking before.

"I have a wife and three daughters who seldom talk about anything else. So I am well aware how important they are."

Larina smiled.

"Then as you understand perhaps you will help me. I have no further need for anything in this house, and so I want to sell everything it contains."

"You will be leaving this house then, when you come back from Sorrento?" Mr. Donaldson asked.

"Yes . . . I will be . . . going away."

"Well we could put the furniture up for auction, or even try to find a buyer among the dealers, but it is going to take time."

He looked around him, then said:

"I wonder if you could show me the rest of the house, Miss Milton?"

"Of course," Larina agreed.

She rose to her feet and led Mr. Donaldson over the house.

There was not a great deal to see.

The mahogany bed and the matching furniture in her mother's room, while attractive, were not valuable.

There was nothing in her own room which was worth more than a few pounds, but the Dining-Room table was good and so were the chairs which her father had said were Hepplewhite.

They were however not fashionable at the moment and there were some pictures on the walls which seemed to interest Mr. Donaldson more.

Finally they went into the tiny Study, and he glanced round quickly, apparently not interested in the books.

"I am afraid that is everything!" Larina said apologetically. "There is practically nothing downstairs in the kitchen. You see, since my father died we have not been able to afford a maid."

She blushed as she spoke, thinking he would find it strange that she had lied to him on his arrival.

"You are living here alone?" he asked.

She nodded.

"I do not like to think of your doing that, Miss Milton," he said. "I should not permit it if it was one of my own daughters. It seems to me that the sooner you get to Sorrento the better!"

He paused, then added with a smile:

"Naturally you cannot go without something to wear and I think I can solve the problem."

"How can you do that?" Larina asked.

"I am going to advance you a hundred pounds, Miss Milton, and while you are away I will sell the contents of your house. If it comes to more than a hundred pounds then I will let you have the balance when you return."

"Supposing it is less?" Larina asked apprehensively.

"I do not think it will be," Mr. Donaldson replied. "It is just a question of finding the right purchasers and that takes time. Some of the things, like the desk in the Sitting-Room, are quite valuable and the sideboard in the Dining-Room is worth perhaps fifteen pounds!"

"Perhaps you should get further advice before you commit yourself," Larina suggested nervously.

"I'll take a gamble on it," Mr. Donaldson smiled.

He sat down as he spoke at the desk in the Study which Larina had used.

It was a sturdy piece of furniture and had none of the elegance of her mother's upstairs.

"If I write you a cheque," Mr. Donaldson said taking a cheque-book out of his pocket, "you'll be able to cash it tomorrow. Could you buy all the clothes you need in three days?"

"Yes, I am sure I could," Larina agreed.

"That will give me time to make the reservations on the boat from Dover to Calais and on the trains that will take you first to Rome and then on to Naples."

"I can hardly believe it is true," Larina exclaimed.

"I'll let you know what time I shall be calling for you on Thursday morning," Mr. Donaldson said. "I have a feeling it will be early."

"I will not mind that."

Mr. Donaldson blotted the cheque.

"If there is anything you want to ask me in the meantime," he said, "you can get in touch with me at this address."

He made as if to take a card from his pocket — then changed his mind and wrote the address down on a piece of paper.

"Just call a messenger," he said, "and I'll come round as quickly as possible."

"I am sure I shall want nothing," Larina replied. "I shall be too busy shopping."

"That's right," Mr. Donaldson smiled. "You enjoy yourself, Miss Milton. I don't think you will want anything very elaborate. Since Mr. Farren has been ill I don't suppose he will be entertaining extensively."

"No, of course not," Larina answered.

"The gardens of the Villa are very beautiful," Mr. Donaldson said. "In fact people say they are the most beautiful gardens in the whole of Southern Italy, and the Villa itself is superb! It was originally the house of a famous Roman Senator, but I expect Mr. Farren will want to tell you about it himself."

"I feel I am dreaming!" Larina said. "This cannot be happening. If you only knew what it meant to me . . ."

She stopped suddenly. She had been on the verge of revealing too much of her private feelings to a stranger.

"I can understand," Mr. Donaldson said. "I often feel like that when I am dealing with Mr. —"

He checked himself and seemed to stumble over the name as he finished: "— Farren and his brothers."

He moved towards the door.

"And now, Miss Milton, if you will excuse me," he said. "I have a lot to do before I call for you on Thursday, and there is not much of today left."

Larina saw him to the door and held out her hand.

"Good-bye, Mr. Donaldson," she said. "Thank you, thank you very much indeed!"

"Good-bye, Miss Milton," he replied gravely.

As he walked away, she saw that he had a motor-car driven by a chauffeur waiting for him a little way down the street.

She stared in surprise.

A motor-car!

There were only a few of them in London and the public looked at them in surprise and even consternation.

Elvin had never mentioned anything about motor-cars when they had been talking together, and she could not imagine him driving one of those ugly vehicles which caused so much dust and frightened the horses.

"The day I have to visit my patients in a motor-car," she had heard her father say often enough, "I will give up my practice! Why, to come hooting up to the door would frighten anyone with a bad heart into having a seizure!"

"They are so nasty and smelly!" Larina's mother had complained.

"Everyone is crazy for speed," Dr. Milton had gone on, "faster trains, faster ships, motor-cars rushing along the roads, running over children and dogs — where will it all end?"

"Where indeed?" his wife echoed with a sigh. "I know of nothing more delightful than driving quietly and with dignity in a comfortable carriage."

But secretly Larina had often longed to go

in a motor-car. Then peeping round the door, as she saw Mr. Donaldson drive off she half wished she could be sitting beside him.

Even the noise the car made as it journeyed down Eaton Terrace had something exciting about it.

But as she closed the door she told herself that for the moment everything seemed exciting.

How could it be possible that she was going to Italy in three days' time?

Italy which she had always longed to see, which she had learnt about, read about and talked about to her father.

And Sorrento of all places!

She had not told Mr. Donaldson because it made her feel shy. But the reason she was particularly interested was that it was near Sorrento that Ulysses was said to have resisted the call of the Sirens. He had plugged the ears of his crew with wax and made them lash him to the mast of the ship so that he should not be enslaved by their voices.

Of all the books that her father had made her read Larina had been most interested in those about Greece.

Dr. Milton had been particularly concerned with archaeological discoveries in Pompeii and Herculaneum and with the tombs that had been recently excavated in Egypt, but he had also encouraged her to study the religions and histories of all the ancient civilizations.

She knew from what she had read that Sorrento was in the Bay of Naples where the rich Romans had built their summer Villas.

But before the Romans, it had been colonised by Greek settlers who were said to have founded the Temple of Athene on the tip of the promontory.

In all her reading of history, the Greeks had thrilled Larina as no other people had been able to do.

She had tried to be enthusiastic about the other cultures and religions which absorbed her father. But the Babylonian and Assyrian gods were heavy and earthy, the Egyptian gods with their animal features grotesque.

The Greeks had no Kings as splendid as the Pharaohs, no pyramids, no Nile to bring fertility to the land.

Yet it seemed to Larina that they had discovered something which was different to all the other civilisations — it was light and was personified in their god, Apollo.

As the god of light, the god of divine radiance, every morning Apollo moved across the sky, intensely virile, flashing with a million points of light, healing everything he touched, germinating the seeds and defying the powers of darkness.

To Larina he became very real.

Even as the Greeks had seen him not only as the sun, but as a perfect man, she had visualised him too, and gradually there had grown up a picture of him in her mind.

He was not only the sun, he was the moon, the planets, the Milky-Way and the stars. He was the sparkle of the waves, the gleam in the eyes. Of all the gods, her books had told her, he was the one who conferred the greatest blessings and was the most generous and the most far-seeing.

What she had loved was when her father had told her that Apollo's constant companion was the dolphin, the sleekest and shiniest of all creatures.

Larina had gone to the Zoo and looked at the dolphins and thought of them as attendant on Apollo, shining as he shone with a light which lit not only the world but men's minds.

She tried to tell her father what she felt and thought he understood.

"I found when I was in Greece," he said, "that at night when Apollo vanishes the Greeks are miserable. I do not believe there are any other people in the world who keep so many lights burning in their houses."

106

He smiled as he went on:

"Even during the brightest days they will light their lamps, when they can barely afford the oil."

He paused before he added more seriously:

"Light is their protection against the evil of darkness."

"Apollo is light," Larina told herself.

If she could not go to Greece before she died, at least in Sorrento she would actually be standing on soil where Greeks had worshipped him.

It seemed to her in the excitement of what she was planning that it would not be Elvin she was meeting in Sorrento, but Apollo, who had been part of her childhood dreams and who as she grew older had in some way been part of the mind she was developing within herself.

That, she knew, was what the Greeks had brought to the world, the development not only of a perfect body, but also of a questing mind, a mind such as she had herself where she believed there were no bounds to knowledge and to reason.

There was however little time for introspection or for thinking too long about Apollo. She had to buy clothes, and for the first time she knew that what she spent would not be extravagant because she would have no sense of guilt about it.

She rose very early the following morning and hurried to the Bank, cashing Mr. Donaldson's cheque for one hundred pounds and drawing out what remained of the small balance which had been dwindling away every week since her return to London.

"I will keep ten pounds for tips and I can spend the rest," she told herself.

There would be no chance of her returning from Sorrento, since the twenty-one days would be up very shortly after she arrived there and after that she would have no further need of money.

She wished she had asked Mr. Donaldson more about the clothes she would need in Sorrento, but told herself he was unlikely to know any more than she did.

She was aware that in the sunshine one needed white or bright colours and there was very little in her existing wardrobe which would be of any use.

Besides with her one hundred pounds she was determined to look her best for Elvin, and perhaps be a worthy visitor to the Villa of which Mr. Donaldson had spoken so warmly.

The difficulty of course was that she had

no time to have anything made.

The best clothes in London from the best dressmakers were designed for each individual customer and were fitted several times and took at least two or three weeks to be completed.

Her mother's best clothes which she wore on special occasions had all been made by a dressmaker in Hanover Square, but even so they had not been very expensive because the Doctor's wife could not have afforded anything extravagant.

Larina went first to Peter Robinson in Regent Street where there were dresses ready made.

She found two light gowns which could be altered by the following day to fit her. They were pretty, light muslins that were not expensive and were in fact the only gowns in the shop that were not much too large in the bust.

"You are very slim, Miss," the fitter said as she pinned away at the superfluous folds of the material.

"I know I am not fashionable," Larina said with a smile.

"I dare say you'll put on a bit as you get older," the woman said comfortingly.

The silhouette popularised by the American Charles Dana Gibson had swept England. His magazine-drawings of lovely women standing with a pronounced forward tilt, had brought into vogue 'the Gibson S bend'!

Larina knew she would never have the ample and protuberant bosom or the definitely curved behind which was accentuated by the swing of the skirt, and often by discreetly hidden little pads.

One thing she was determined not to buy were the boned, high necks which most ladies affected in the daytime and which Larina knew were very uncomfortable.

Instead she chose gowns which had a piece of soft muslin round the neck which ended as a bow in the front or alternatively a bow at the back. It was modest, but definitely not boned.

"It would be too restrictive in the heat anyway," she told herself, feeling a little guilty that she had no desire to be fashionable.

Then as she was wondering where she should buy her evening-gowns, she remembered that she and her mother when they had been in Switzerland had been looking at the pictures in *'The Ladies Journal'* and had seen some very attractive designs by Paul Poiret.

Underneath them was written:

'This French designer is trying to change the trend of women's clothes to what he calls a more graceful, flowing look. His new ideas, like his new creations, are causing a sensation in Paris as well as in London.'

"There would be no harm in looking!" Larina told herself.

She knew that Poiret's shop was in Berkeley Street, and with a feeling of being utterly reckless she took a hackney-carriage instead of trying to get there by omnibus.

Ordinarily she had been far too shy and too nervous to enter the luxurious precincts of such a shop by herself, but now that she had no future she had developed a courage she had never had before.

If people were surprised at her behaviour it did not matter; if people criticised her she would not be here long enough to hear it! Even if she did something outrageous it would be forgotten in three weeks' time when she was dead.

Quite boldly, not even worrying about her somewhat dowdy appearance, she entered the shop and asked to see some of their models.

"We have very few models to show at the

moment, Madam," a very superior looking Vendeuse told her. "Monsieur Poiret's new collection from Paris will be shown next week. At the moment we really only have the garments that are in the sale."

"In the sale!" Larina exclaimed.

She realised this meant the clothes were ready and could be altered to fit her.

She would not be told, as she had half-expected, that everything would take a long time to be made for her.

She felt afterwards it had been an inspiration, a stroke of good fortune, that she had been brave enough to enter Poiret's.

She came away with two evening-gowns and two for the day besides a travelling outfit.

When she explained to the Vendeuse that she was leaving for Italy on Friday, perhaps because of the excitement in her voice or perhaps because she looked very young and, although she was not aware of it, rather helpless, the woman ceased to appear superior and became warm and friendly.

Finally dropping all barriers she asked:

"How much have you to spend?"

"I have nearly a hundred pounds for everything!" Larina said.

They made out a budget together; so much for hats; she would need only one large shady one for the sun and she could change the ribbons around to match her various gowns.

So much for shoes: she would need white ones for the daytime and a pair of satin slippers to go with the evening gowns.

For gloves she could manage with what she had already, and all the rest could be expended on the exciting, original, delightful gowns which, as the Vendeuse pointed out, Mr. Poiret might have designed specially for her.

Larina learnt that he did not like the Gibson S bend. He liked gowns that flowed, that had a rhythm about them, and those were the sort of gowns into which Larina was fitted.

There was one of white which was made of chiffon, another in the pale pink which made her think of almond blossom.

The evening-gowns had chiffon scarves to match, and all of them seemed to fall in a fluid line which reminded her of the movement of the wind in long grass.

"You look lovely, Madam, you do really!" the Vendeuse exclaimed when finally the last gown was fitted and she was promised they would all be delivered late on Wednesday evening.

Looking in the mirror Larina had no

doubt that they did become her better than anything she had ever worn in her life before.

They brought out the lights in her very fair hair, the light in the grey of her eyes which sometimes held a touch of green in them, and they accentuated the whiteness of her skin.

"You have been so kind," she said impulsively to the Vendeuse, "I still cannot believe that I could have been so brave as to come into this shop alone."

"It has been a real pleasure!" the Vendeuse said with a note of sincerity in her voice. "I only wish I could come with you to Italy and see you wearing them."

"I wish you could too," Larina answered.

"Never mind, I know how admired you will be," the Vendeuse said, "and that is a satisfaction in itself!"

Larina smiled. She was sure that Elvin would admire her and she wanted to look nice for him.

She remembered the little compliments he had paid her. Then she remembered the biggest compliment of all, when he had said he wanted her to be with him when his 'spirit took wings'.

Now it would not be his spirit which was flying away into the unknown, but hers.

'In Sorrento I shall be flying into the light not into the darkness,' Larina thought, 'and with Elvin there I shall not be afraid.'

Chapter Four

Wynstan had travelled from Paris to Rome and from Rome to Naples in an irritated frame of mind.

He had, as he had expected, enjoyed himself on the *'Kaiser Wilhelm der Grosse'* with the alluring Countess of Glencairn.

He had known when he went down to the big Dining-Saloon the first night that he had not been mistaken in thinking that she found him as attractive as he found her.

Her dark eyes lit up when he appeared and her lips pouted provocatively, and long before the evening was over he knew they were all set to enjoy an *affaire de coeur* in which the French could indulge with such lightness that it was in fact like a *soufflé surprise*.

Having been amused by women of many nations, Wynstan found the French more sophisticated and more civilised in their attitude to love than any others.

They approached it like an epicurean discovering a new and strange dish, savoured it carefully and without hurry so that the full flavour, the underlying succulent taste, was fully appreciated.

English women, Wynstan thought, were always so deadly serious in their love affairs. It was invariably a case of 'Will you love me for ever?' 'Is this the first time you have felt as you do now?'

There was always at the back of their minds the idea that love must be a permanency rather than just a 'will o' the wisp' which could fly away overnight but which nevertheless was an enchantment for the moment.

Yvette Glencairn was experienced in the ancient science of fascinating a man, and Wynstan, who thought he knew every move in the game, was entranced to find that there were some new moves which definitely added to his education.

Because she was French and clever at keeping not one man but many under her spell, Yvette was always charming to her husband, which so often the English forgot was important when the other man was only a case of *pour passer le temps*.

The Earl hailed Wynstan with pleasure and talked to him of horses and the days when he had been Master of Hounds.

They speculated and argued as to who was likely to win the Derby and the other classic races in England that Season.

Wynstan had sat with the Glencairns at meals, and they had often come to his cabin after luncheon or dinner was over.

But when the Earl had retired to bed and the rest of the ship's passengers were settling down for the night, it was then that Yvette, in a diaphanous and very revealing rest-gown, would open the door of Wynstan's cabin to find him waiting for her.

She was enticing, exciting and very satisfying, and when she pleaded with him to stay with them in Paris, he had been sorely tempted to postpone his journey to Sorrento for several days.

He was well aware how many friends he would find in Paris at this time of the year.

The chestnuts would be coming out in the Champs Élysées, the flower-sellers' baskets would be filled with parma violets, there would be the smell of spring in the air, and Maxim's would be gayer than ever.

As his mother had found out by some mysterious means of her own, he had when he was last in Paris, spent a considerable amount of time with the successor of the *grandes cocottes Parisiennes* of the '90s, the glamorous Gaby Deslys.

She was the theatrical figure of whom all Paris was talking and it was obvious to Wynstan, as it was to all her other admirers, that her success would be phenomenal.

She had none of the beauty which Wynstan usually sought in women. But her cherubic face, her eyes warm and enticing beneath their heavy lids, her crimson lips that were always parted in a smile which revealed sensuality, gaiety and good nature, made her somehow different from anyone else.

She was audacious, bizarre, at times vulgar, and she looked like a bird of Paradise — not only on the stage, when she wore very little except feathers and pearls but in the restaurants, and also by some mysterious chemistry of her own in bed!

She had a vitality which made everything she did seem sensual, and yet the more luxurious and the more scandalous she was the more people loved her.

From the very moment she appeared she seemed to personify Paris itself, and when she had acted in London the previous year, the newspapers wrote of her as being *'la Vie Parisienne'*, and meant it!

It would be amusing to see Gaby again, Wynstan told himself, and there were a great many other friends he knew would welcome him with open arms. But he had promised Harvey he would keep Larina Milton from making trouble and already the election in America was gathering momentum.

The *'Kaiser Wilhelm der Grosse'* had not equalled her regular run from New York to Southampton which was five days, twenty-two hours and forty-five minutes. Instead owing to the weather she was forty hours late.

It had taken another day and night before he got away from Cherbourg and it was very late on the 8th April by the time Wynstan reached Paris.

This was the quickest way he could reach Rome but he was delighted when he found that he could stay the night in Paris before catching an express the following morning.

Unfortunately he missed the express.

It was understandable as he did not reach his Suite in the Ritz Hotel until six o'clock in the morning after what had seemed a night of laughter — sparkling and frothy as a glass of champagne!

Gaby ablaze with feathers and jewels had danced on one of the tables at Maxim's, and after Wynstan had taken her home he had known there would be no chance of his catching the express which left the Gare de l'Est at a quarter to seven.

What was more the next Rome express from Paris did not leave until the following day. The alternatives were slow trains, and frequent changes which would not get him there any quicker.

He felt guilty!

Then he told himself there would be no indiscreet American newspapers in Sorrento, and if Elvin's girl-friend had to cool her heels a little she might be all the more eager to settle for a reasonable sum.

He had thought about Larina while crossing the Atlantic, and he had come to the conclusion that Harvey was wrong and that it was impossible that she should be having Elvin's child.

Elvin had never been like that — or had he?

There had been no woman in his life — that Wynstan thought he knew — but then he told himself he had been out of touch with Elvin for long periods of time.

When they were together they had an affinity which was closer than anything he enjoyed with his two elder brothers; but after all he had been abroad so much that Elvin might have developed interests of which he had no idea.

There always seemed to Wynstan to be something of Sir Galahad about Elvin.

Because he had been weak and sickly even as a child, he read a great deal more than the rest of the family, and when he talked to Elvin it had usually been on philosophy or psychology and they seldom touched on modern or common-place topics.

But that was not to say, Wynstan told himself, that Elvin had not developed an interest in women of which he was not aware.

It was obvious from Larina's cable that she had meant something in his life.

For instance what had he promised her and what had he said in his letters? There were no answers to his questions except those he would not accept.

When finally Wynstan set off for Naples he began to feel angry.

If this woman had hurt Elvin in any way he would strangle her!

Elvin was someone special in his life, someone whose image he could not bear to have spoiled or defamed.

It was this which had made him agree to go to Europe rather than Harvey's almost hysterical fear that his election campaign might be damaged.

Wynstan was fond of his oldest brother, but he saw quite clearly his ruthlessness, his egotism, his insatiable ambition for power and importance.

He did not criticise, he merely accepted it as being what Harvey was; but where Elvin was concerned his feelings were very different.

Elvin was a part of his heart which Wynstan never revealed to anyone else.

Everything that was idealistic in Wynstan was concealed under a cynical and detached attitude which women found irresistible.

Because they could not capture him, could not pin him down, and make him their captive, they pursued him frantically and relentlessly.

The amused twinkle which was never far from his blue eyes drove them crazy, while to Harvey and Gary he was an enigmatic figure whom they decried because they could not understand him.

"Wynstan is just a play-boy! He has not a thought in his head beyond amusing himself," Harvey said often enough, and knew even as he spoke it was untrue.

Wynstan stood apart from the family and his mother knew it, which was why she claimed in all truth that he was exceptional. The rules and regulations she insisted on for the rest of her children did not apply to him.

The train was due to arrive in Naples in the afternoon.

It had been very hot since early in the morning when they had changed trains at Rome.

Wynstan's valet had laid out for him in his sleeping-compartment a white tussore suit and a fine linen shirt which made him look even more elegant than usual.

Wynstan bought his suits in London, his shirts in Paris, his shoes in Italy, and his cuff-links at Tiffany's in New York.

However he wore his clothes with an ease and elegance which made them seem so much a part of himself that people did not notice them but only him.

It was seven years since he had been to Naples and since he had stayed in his grandfather's Villa at Sorrento.

He had forgotten, he thought, that Naples — nicknamed 'the devil's paradise' — was mysterious. And he told himself as the train steamed into the station that it was one of the few cities of ancient pre-Christian times that had not perished but had survived on the surface of the modern world.

He was met at the station by a Courier who had been notified of his arrival by Mr. Donaldson.

He led Wynstan away from the bustle and noise of the station to say apologetically:

"*Scusi, Signor,* but I could not find you a car at such short notice."

He thought he saw Wynstan's expression darken and went on hastily:

"I thought a comfortable carriage, *Signor,* with fast horses was better than an uncomfortable car which undoubtedly will break down on the journey to Sorrento."

There was something so ingenuous in his explanation that Wynstan smiled.

"I am in no great hurry," he said.

As he drove off, leaving his valet to cope with the luggage and follow him in another carriage, he thought that was the truth.

He was in no hurry to reach Sorrento and the problems that awaited him there, and now as the excellent horses carried him through the beautiful city he began to relax and look at his surroundings.

The houses with their elaborate porticos, the Castel Dell'Oro, the baroque Churches, Palazzos, the Piazza Pebiscito and the splendour of Naples made him remember how it had been founded by the Greeks who settled in Cumal in 730 B.C.

But what he had forgotten besides the beauty of Naples with its narrow steps ascending towards the sky, its alleys, its subterranean dwellings, and its Port filled with ships and small boats, was the quality of the air.

Wynstan drew in his breath and thought he would have recognised it with his eyes shut.

There was something different about it, an air that could be found nowhere else. Just as when he had his first view of the sea, it had a transparent luminosity that was also different.

As soon as they were outside the city he saw Vesuvius rising immediately from the coastal plain, its wooded slopes towering high above the road down which he was travelling.

Now he leant back and forgot everything except the beauty of the flowers, the shrubs, the trees in blossom and the picturesqueness of the small villages where half the population seemed to be sitting out in the sunshine drinking wine.

And where inevitably there was the sound of music.

"How could I have been so stupid as not to come here more often?" Wynstan asked himself and he wished that when he reached the Villa he could be alone there.

Because he felt suddenly reluctant to face anything that might spoil the loveliness of the blue sea, the vivid sky and the vibrant quality of the air, he stopped the carriage at the *Castellammare di Stabia.*

There he sat outside a small Inn and ordered a bottle of the local wine.

The Italian coachman was delighted. He

put hay bags over the noses of the two horses and disappeared to find friends at the back of the Inn.

Ahead, Wynstan knew, was the most beautiful drive on earth and he thought that perhaps the glass of wine would sharpen his appreciation of what he had believed as a child was the road which led to El Dorado.

He had always been surprised that his grandfather, who had seemed to most people a rather frightening, overpowering man, should have had the imagination and the vision to create anything so beautiful as the Villa where he had spent the last years of his life.

He had rebuilt it to the exact design of what it was believed to have looked like in Roman times.

There had remained some of the magnificent mosaic floors, a number of pillars, a few broken walls, and of course the foundations.

Following the lines of these and collecting everything in the neighbourhood which might at some time have been remotely connected with the Villa, old Mr. Vanderfeld had created a Palace of beauty that was unsurpassed in the whole of Italy.

What was more, and this had surprised his family more than anything, he had made the garden a dream of loveliness.

It had required vision and imagination and Wynstan had often thought as he grew older that he resembled his grandfather more than his father.

There had been a poetry in his grandfather that had been transmitted to Elvin and himself, but not to Harvey or Gary.

His wine finished, reluctantly Wynstan resumed his journey, followed by the admiring glances of the dark-eyed *Signorinas* gathered round the fountain in the village.

The water of *Castellammare di Stabia* had been famous since Roman times, and there was the Grotto in the hills which had been there long before the Romans.

They drove on and now the sea was suffused with a golden light which came with the setting of the sun.

The Villa Arcadia was at the actual point where the mountains gave way to the undoubtedly fertile *Peano di Sorrento*, a natural terrace some 300 feet high, falling in sheer cliffs to the Bay of Naples.

There were, as Wynstan knew, special steps built down to the sea where there was a private jetty and where he expected to find his motor-boat.

It had been built for him in Monte Carlo and he had cabled the ship-builders to send it to Sorrento so that it would be there by the time he arrived.

He was looking forward to seeing it. He had owned motor-boats before, but this was a very special one and built to his own design.

He hoped he would have the opportunity to get away on his own and try it out in the Bay.

The plain of Sorrento was an unbroken expanse of luxuriant green except for the white walls of an occasional villa and the Church towers and domes capped with multicoloured majolica.

Everywhere there were orange and lemon trees, burdened with their fruit, vineyards, walnut and fig trees, cherries and pomegranates and tropical flowers.

The horses turned in at the wrought iron gates which Wynstan's grandfather had copied from the gates of one of the famous Palaces in Naples.

They were magnificent, emblazoned with gold and flanked on either side with stone griffons which had once stood in the garden of an ancient Temple before it was forgotten and allowed to fall into decay.

It was a short drive rising on either side of a stone fountain surrounded by yellow azaleas.

At the front door there was a balustraded terrace covered with climbing geraniums and roses.

'It is lovelier than I remembered!' Wynstan thought to himself and stepped out to be greeted by a number of Italian servants.

The entrance-hall was cool, the pattern on the floor was a replica of one of the mosaics discovered in Herculaneum.

The marble pillars, the painted ceilings, the view from the windows, all brought the whole enchantment of the Villa back to Wynstan's mind.

He could remember running through the house as a child and hearing his own laughter echoing and re-echoing down the marble passages. The golden sunshine outside in the garden had warmed and invigorated him so that he felt free and untrammelled as he had never been again in the whole of his life.

"You had a good journey, *Signor?*" the elderly Italian who appeared to be in charge was asking him.

"Yes, thank you, a very good journey," Wynstan replied.

"You require wine or refreshment, *Signor?*"

"Not for the moment," Wynstan answered. "Where is Miss Milton?"

"You will find her in the garden, *Signor*. The *Signorina* arrived three days ago. She has spent all her time in the garden and she finds it very beautiful — *bellissimo!* We are glad she is pleased!"

"I will find her," Wynstan said.

Bare-headed he walked out into a blaze of colour. The terraces which climbed the hill to the right of the Villa looked like the Hanging Gardens of Babylon.

The scent of tuberoses, lilacs and lilies filled the air, and under the olive trees sloping down to the plain, the grass was carpeted with hyacinths. Everywhere there was a profusion of tulips, peonies and daffodils.

The almond trees which were the first to bloom had already shed their petals, Wynstan noticed, and there was a carpet of pink and white blossoms beneath them.

The branches of the Judas tree were purple against the sky, the laburnums cascaded like golden rain, and beyond them the mimosa was a yellow cloud.

He looked around and realised that as the sun was sinking, the flame-coloured azaleas were echoed by what appeared to be flames of fire rising in the sky.

He moved forward, knowing almost instinctively where Larina Milton would be at this time of the evening.

Always at sunset anyone who stayed in the Villa climbed up the twisting stone steps of the hanging gardens to where high above the Villa on a promontory overlooking the sea there was an ancient Temple.

It had been built, Wynstan's grandfather had discovered, by Greeks, and he had restored it without knowing to which god it was dedicated.

Then in the last year of his life, when they were digging to extend the garden further, they had found a statue.

Time and weather had refined the whiteness of the marble, rain and sun had brought colour to it so that it almost resembled flesh.

It was not greatly damaged, except that it had lost its arms and the features of the face were obliterated, but it had a beauty and a grace that was breathtaking.

The legs were veiled with a loose garment which began below the hips, the exquisite curves of the breasts and the lines of the lower body were undamaged. The whole statue made anyone who looked at it draw in their breath as if they had never believed such beauty existed.

"It is Aphrodite!" Wynstan's grandfather had declared. "The goddess of beauty, love and reproduction!"

"How can you be sure of that?" Wynstan had asked.

He had been fifteen at the time and pleased because his grandfather talked to him as if he were a grown man.

"Can you not see just by looking at her, that she could be nothing else?" the old man had enquired. "She was born in the sea-foam and she stood here in her Temple overlooking the sea, bringing happiness and prosperity to those who toiled on it."

Wynstan had looked for a long time at the goddess whom his grandfather had set on a marble pedestal.

He had grown lilies on either side of her because lilies, he said, were the right flowers for Aphrodite.

"Why particularly?" Wynstan enquired.

"Because they are always the symbol of purity," his grandfather had answered. "To the Greeks the goddess of love was not a many-breasted matron, but a young virgin rising out of the waves."

He had paused to stare at the statue of Aphrodite. Her head was turned to the right of her body, and although she had no remaining features it was somehow easy to imagine them.

The little straight nose, the wide, innocent eyes, the softly curved lips!

"In a sense the Greeks invented virginity for their goddesses," old Mr. Vanderfeld went on. "To them it was fresh, clean and full of promise like the coming of each day."

He saw that Wynstan was listening intently and continued:

"Aphrodite was a grey-eyed goddess, untouched and part of every man's dreams. She brought all that was beautiful and perfect to those who worshipped her so that never again could they be content with the second-rate."

He smiled at the school-boy.

"When she went to the Assembly of the Immortals the gods were silent with admiration, and Homer wrote that each wished in his heart to take her as a wife and lead her to his abode."

Everything his grandfather had told him came back to Wynstan now, and he thought as he climbed up the stone steps that when he grew old this was where he would live out his life and where he would die.

In the meantime, although he dedicated so much of his life to the pursuit of love, he had not yet found any woman that his grandfather would have described as Aphrodite.

Those he had loved and who had loved

him had never been able to touch something secret in his heart that had been engendered all those years ago when his grandfather had spoken to him of love.

He had been continually infatuated, excited and delighted by women, but always there had come a moment when he knew that he no longer needed them and they no longer meant anything to him.

They were like the butterflies still hovering over the flowers but which by the morning would no longer exist, and their place would be taken by others as colourful and as dispensable as they were themselves.

The sky was growing more brilliant every moment, the sunset so vivid, so dazzling, that it was hard to look at it.

Then as he reached the last steps which led to the Temple itself, Wynstan realised that he had been right in thinking that this was where he would find Larina Milton.

There was a woman standing against the marble balustrade looking out over the sea. It was difficult to see her distinctly because the sunset was so blinding that she was little more than a silhouette against it.

She was wearing white, and her hair was very pale gold, and yet the light from the sky made it shimmer as if with tiny tongues of flame.

She must have heard his footsteps for even as he stepped onto the mosaic floor of the Temple she turned and for one incredible moment he thought that she was Aphrodite!

Larina had been disappointed when she arrived at the Villa Arcadia to find that Elvin was not already there waiting for her, but she had been entranced by the drive from Naples and the incredible beauty of the Villa.

The Courier who had accompanied her on the journey was an elderly man who told her he had once been a schoolmaster. He had explained very clearly the history of every place they passed.

He was however more interested in Venice than in other parts of Italy and it was hard for Larina to keep him on the subjects she wished to learn about when he was longing to describe to her the glories of San Marco and the tragedy of the Venetian decline.

Nevertheless he told her many myths and legends of Southern Italy and when he said good-bye she felt sorry to lose him.

"Are you going back straight away?" she asked in surprise.

"They expect me in London, Miss Milton."

"Then thank you very much for looking after me."

"It has been a great pleasure," he answered, "and I say that in all sincerity! It is not often I take on a journey anyone who has your enquiring mind and your love of antiquities!"

"I can see already that the Villa is breath-takingly beautiful!" Larina said.

He had told her how it had been restored in what was believed to be its original design.

"Mr. er . . . er . . . Farren went to endless trouble to have the experts' opinion on every room, every floor and every ceiling."

There was a perceptible pause before the Courier pronounced Mr. Farren's name which Larina had noticed on other occasions, and she wondered why everyone seemed to find it difficult to say the word 'Farren'.

"Perhaps it is because it begins with an 'F'," she told herself. "Some people might have as much difficulty with their 'Fs' as with their 'Ths'."

But it seemed strange that both Mr. Donaldson and the Courier should have the same impediment.

However her curiosity in that respect was quickly swept away by her excitement over the Villa and its garden.

The garden particularly had been unlike anything else she had ever seen or imagined.

It was easy here to imagine Apollo as she had never been able to imagine him before, and she longed impatiently to talk about him to Elvin.

She was certain he would know more than she did about the 'far-shining one', 'the friend of Zeus', 'the giver of music and song'.

Nothing the Greeks ever created, Larina told herself, could have been more magnificent than this god who tore the darkness from the human soul and lit it with divine light.

Her first evening at the Villa she had on the servants' suggestion gone up to the Temple to see the sunset.

Watching the glory of it she had almost believed that she saw Apollo in the dazzling light which turned the sea to gold and touched every mountain and beach with a light that was indescribable.

Then, as gradually the sun vanished and the darkness was encroaching, she felt there was a strange glitter high in the air, a mysterious quivering, the beating of silver wings and the whirring of silver wheels.

That, she told herself, was how the

Greeks had known Apollo was near and she was certain at that moment he was close to her.

It was not the same ecstasy that she had felt at the Serpentine when she had been aware of life; it was something outside herself, and it was so perfect, so exquisite, that she wanted to catch it and make it hers.

Then with the coming of darkness Apollo had gone, but she could think of nothing else.

She had not felt lonely the next day. She had been waited on by the warm-hearted smiling Italians who had looked at her with dark, liquid eyes and tried in their own way to make her happy.

She thought as she walked about the garden that a strange music accompanied her, not only from the buzz of the bees and the song of the birds, but also as if she heard some celestial song on the air itself.

All that evening she had dreamt of Apollo.

She found books in the Villa which were written about the myths and legends of the Greeks and Romans in which there were references to him.

But they were only words, and she had but to go into the garden to feel that his very presence over-shadowed everything.

She began to be aware of an expectant quietness like the presence of an unexplained mystery which would shortly be revealed.

In one of the books she had read some verses translated from Sophocles and she found herself repeating some words of it as she walked alone:

"He who has won some new splendour
    dour
Rides on the air,
Borne upwards on the winds of his
    human vigour."

'Only Apollo,' she thought, 'would ride on the air.'

She felt as if she could speak to him as the evening breeze from the sea moved her hair and touched the softness of her cheeks.

Because she did not wish to miss a moment of the sunset or the first shimmering stars that followed it, she had changed for dinner early, putting on her white gown because she had worn her pink one the night before.

Throwing the long chiffon scarf over one shoulder in an unconscious imitation of the Greeks, she walked up to the Temple to stand waiting; almost as one would wait for the curtain to rise in a theatre.

Tonight the sunset was even lovelier than it had been before: the gold was more gold, the crimson more crimson, the blue more blue; and the shining glory of it seemed to blaze as the legends said the whole island of Delos had done when the goddess Leto gave birth to her son Apollo.

Larina felt herself caught up in the ecstasy of it and the music she had heard all day was beating in her ears.

She heard a step behind her and turned her head.

Her eyes were still dazzled from the setting sun, and yet under the shadows of the Temple she could see someone standing. The light from the sky touched his face and as it did so she thought with a sudden leap of her heart that it was Apollo who stood there!

For a long, long moment there was silence, a silence that was not oppressive, merely as if nature stood still and the earth stopped moving.

Then in a voice that sounded strange to himself Wynstan said:

"You are Miss Milton?"

He knew as his voice died away that Larina had difficulty in answering him. Then she said, stammering a little over the words:

"Y-yes . . . who . . . are you?"

He moved closer to her and now he could see why for the moment he had thought she was Aphrodite.

She was very slim, in fact the same height as the goddess that stood beside them on a pedestal. The folds of the scarf she wore over her shoulder were Grecian, so was her gown flowing to her feet.

It was unfashionable, and yet at the same time so utterly and completely right that it was impossible to think of her wearing anything else.

He reached her side and saw that the eyes she raised to his were grey, and her hair swept back from an oval forehead was pale gold but without the tongues of fire that had been there when he first saw her.

She was not like any woman he had ever seen before. Yet there was a rightness about her he could not explain even to himself, except that she seemed part of the Temple, part of the garden, and part of the sun which was sinking into the sea.

"I am Elvin's brother — Wynstan."

"Is Elvin here?"

There was a lilt, an eagerness in her voice.

"I am afraid not. I am his advance guard, so to speak!"

There was a pause, as if neither of them

could think what to say, before Wynstan asked:

"I hope you have not been very lonely? I understand you arrived three days ago."

"I have not been lonely; it is so beautiful, so unbelievably, incredibly lovely!"

"That is what I have always thought," he said. "When I was a child I spent my holidays here with my grandfather."

"I cannot understand why Elvin did not tell me about it."

"I am not sure if he ever came here."

"But why not?"

"Elvin was ill even as a child, and my mother did not wish him to travel in case it proved too much for him."

"What a pity!" Larina said. "He would have loved it! And I thought there would be so much he would be able to tell me that I want to know."

"Perhaps I can answer your questions in his place?" Wynstan suggested.

"They are not exactly questions," Larina replied.

Then as if she felt she had said too much she said quickly:

"Have you come from America?"

"Yes."

"And Elvin is well enough to travel? I could hardly believe it when Mr. Donaldson told me he wanted me to meet him here."

"You were not certain he would come?" Wynstan asked.

She looked away from him out to sea, and he had the feeling she was puzzling how to answer his question.

Here was something he did not understand. She had said quite clearly in her cable: 'Come to me as you promised.' Having said that why should she be surprised that Elvin was ready to oblige her?

"You knew Elvin when he was in Switzerland?" he asked after a moment.

"Yes, we were at the Sanatorium together."

"You were a patient?"

"No, I was there with my mother."

"I hope she is better."

"She died."

"I am sorry to hear that," Wynstan said. "Was that after Elvin had left?"

"Yes, two weeks later."

"It must have been a shock for you, but perhaps you really expected it?"

"No, I hoped she could be cured. Dr. Heinrich has a great reputation for effecting cures."

"So I have heard," Wynstan agreed.

"And if Elvin is better," Larina said, "as he told me he was in a letter he wrote to me after he arrived in New York, then it is entirely due to Dr. Heinrich."

"Yes, of course."

The sun had now finally disappeared below the horizon, and it was just that moment of dusk, pale blue and purple, when the first stars are faint but twinkling, their light growing stronger as the darkness deepens.

Larina looked out to sea and Wynstan could see her small straight nose silhouetted against the sky.

Once again he wondered if she was real. There was something insubstantial and ethereal about her, something which made him think of his dreams of Aphrodite when he was a boy.

Then she looked at him and said:

"I expect you want to go back to the Villa. It will soon be time for dinner and you must be hungry after your journey."

He felt as if she was saying one thing, while at the same time her thoughts were elsewhere. They moved across the marble-floor and found the steps which led down into the garden below.

"Be careful!" Wynstan warned. "It is easy to slip, and this path is very steep."

There was still sufficient light for them to see their way.

The azaleas were already scented shadows and the cypress trees were sharp points rising above their heads.

Larina's gown gleamed white. She seemed to move instinctively without hesitation, and her footfalls were so light that Wynstan walking behind felt almost as if she floated down.

The lights from the Villa were warm, golden and welcoming as they stepped into the marble hall.

"If you will excuse me," Wynstan said formally, "I will go and change. I will not be long."

"I will wait in the Drawing-Room," Larina answered.

She moved away from him down the marble passage to the big Drawing-Room with square windows overlooking the bay on one side and the garden on the other.

It was full of exquisite pieces of furniture that had delighted her ever since she had arrived. She felt they had all been chosen not primarily because they were valuable but because each one was just right for the Villa.

They were not antiques of ancient Rome, of course, but they were classical in their taste; their beauty was something which had been handed down through the centuries and had nothing to do with what was momentarily fashionable.

In the room great pots of arum lilies scented the air and there were fragments of Greek and Roman statuary which must have been found locally.

There was the head of what Larina suspected was a Gladiator, a vase which was broken and yet was so exquisitely beautiful in its proportions that it must be unique.

There were urns and plates, and the marble hand of a child which had existed for centuries long after its owner had grown up and died of old age.

It was all fascinating to look at, but now for the first time since she came to the Villa Larina did not notice her surroundings but sat thinking of the man who must be a part-owner of it.

Mr. Donaldson had said that the Villa belonged to the family, and the family meant Elvin, his three brothers, his sister and his mother.

How strange that they so seldom came here, she thought, and that Elvin had never seen this exquisite family property which she was sure would have filled him with delight.

How could he not have felt part of the life that was pulsating in the beautiful garden? Or part of the sea and the sky that was bluer and more translucent than any sky she had ever imagined?

Then, as if all the time her thoughts had been drawing her in that direction, she thought of Elvin's brother and how for one incredible moment she had thought as she saw him that he must be Apollo.

With the light of the setting sun on his face he had looked exactly as she had always imagined Apollo would look.

There had been a strength besides beauty about him. His clear-cut features, his deep-set eyes and his fair hair brushed back from a square forehead might have served as a model for any of the statues of Apollo that Larina had seen illustrated.

When they had reached the hall she looked at him and realised he had a resemblance to Elvin, or rather, because he was the elder, Elvin resembled him.

But Elvin had been thin, emaciated by his disease, while his brother seemed to glow with health and vigour.

"I had not thought that any man could be so handsome!" Larina told herself.

As he advanced towards her in the Temple, she had had an almost irresistible impulse to kneel at his feet, to worship as the Greeks had worshipped the giver of light.

She told herself that it was going to be difficult to talk to him naturally, to discuss commonplace things, to speak of his voyage from America and her own from London.

Then she told herself he would think it very strange if instead she spoke to him of his life on Olympus, of how he ruled the world by the power of his beauty.

'He would think me mad!' Larina reflected with a smile and knew she must be very careful, very careful indeed, in what she said to him.

Chapter Five

Wynstan came down to breakfast and entered the Dining-Room with its fine plaques decorated with the heads of Roman Emperors which had been found amongst the foundations of the Villa.

The servants hurried to bring him coffee and food, and as he looked out at the sunshine he was glad not to be in New York.

He wondered how Harvey was faring and realised yesterday had been Election day.

He could imagine the crowds, the turmoil, the noise, the violence, the heart-ache and the bitter disappointment of the unsuccessful candidate.

He had a feeling that, however optimistic Harvey might be, Theodore Roosevelt would be re-elected.

He had his enemies — at the same time people looked to him for stability and that was something that was going to count in this particular election.

However, if Harvey did lose, he could not ascribe it to any trouble that Larina had made for him.

Thinking of her, Wynstan could not

imagine her making trouble for anyone.

He had thought as they sat at dinner last night that she was different from any woman he had ever met before.

It was not only her looks, which still made him think of the statue of Aphrodite, but also the way she behaved when she was alone with him.

Wynstan had realised, after he had changed and come downstairs to find her waiting in the Drawing-Room, that she was a lady and it was therefore an insult that they should have asked her to come to the Villa un-chaperoned.

But Harvey had been so convinced that she was a golddigger, a brazen hussy who had got her claws into Elvin because he was rich, that Wynstan had not stopped to think that she might turn out to be very different from the image his brother had created.

Yet he thought it extraordinary that she had accepted Elvin's invitation. She could have refused to set out on the journey accompanied only by a Courier, or she might have insisted on bringing a Chaperon with her.

He did not realise that when he went to change before dinner Larina had thought much the same thing.

The question of a Chaperon had simply

not arisen in her mind, when she expected she was meeting Elvin at the Villa.

She longed to see him, she had a deep affection for him; but she had never thought of him as a man such as her mother had warned her about, or in whose company she was well aware she should be strictly chaperoned.

But although she had thought of Wynstan as a god, he was still a man, still disturbingly masculine, and when twenty minutes later he came into the Drawing-Room wearing his evening-clothes she thought it would be impossible for any man to look more elegant or more attractive.

"I should not be here alone," she told herself. "Mama would be shocked!"

Then she thought that perhaps as Wynstan was an American he would not realise that she was defying the conventions of society.

"And even if I am," Larina asked herself, "what does it matter?"

They sat down to a delicious meal, for as Larina had already found, the Chef in the Villa was outstanding and his dishes were so novel and unusual that they were a delight in themselves.

Before Wynstan arrived, when she had been alone she had, of course, talked to the

Italians who waited on her, who had explained to her the dishes and were delighted that she appreciated them.

She had learnt that Naples was famous for its spaghetti in all forms and that *Maccheroni alla Napoletana* was spaghetti served with sauce made from a special plum-shaped tomato and grated cheese.

But what Larina had enjoyed most had been the delicious fresh fish. The Italian Butler had told her that she must visit the fish-markets where she would see every variety from the little silver-blue anchovies to a gigantic octopus.

The Chef at the Villa cooked *trigla* or red mullet superbly and also the *spigola* or sea bass of the Mediterranean which Larina learnt had no English equivalent.

Wynstan was offered grilled *tonna* or tuna fish, for breakfast which the cook had decorated with scampi.

He had just helped himself from a silver dish when Larina came in from the garden.

She was wearing one of the thin muslins she had bought from Paul Poiret. It was of a very soft green, the colour of the first buds of spring and her hair looked like the pale morning sun.

"You are early!" he exclaimed rising to his feet.

"I have been up for a long time," she answered in her musical voice. "I could not bear to miss . . . anything."

There was something in the way she spoke which made Wynstan look at her speculatively.

Then one of the servants pulled out a chair from the table and she seated herself opposite him. As she did so, he thought of how long they had talked last night.

He had found it a new experience to have a woman listening to him wide-eyed, as if he was the source of all wisdom, and without making any attempt to draw his attention to herself.

After the flirtatious enticements of Yvette Glencairn, who could not say 'good-evening' without suggesting a *double entendre* he found that Larina's grey eyes fixed on his face spurred him to an eloquence he did not know he possessed.

They talked, as was inevitable, of the Villa, of the Greeks who had built there and the Romans who came after them.

He told her how his grandfather had found the site quite by chance when he was looking for somewhere to retire; how he had become obsessed with the idea of re-building on the old foundations; and how every expert in Italy had come to Sorrento to advise him.

Larina listened wide-eyed.

Then when Wynstan told her how his grandfather had sought all over the country for the furniture, the pictures and pieces of statuary to decorate not only the house but also the garden, she had said as if it suddenly struck her:

"It must have been very expensive!"

Her words stopped Wynstan as effectively as if she had slammed a door in his face.

'So she is thinking of money!' he thought.

Because he had been carried away by a subject which interested him, he had revealed all too clearly that expense was of little importance where the family was concerned.

Harvey would have sneered at him for being so inept and because he felt he must somehow explain away what had already been said he replied:

"Labour is very cheap in Italy. It would naturally cost a great deal more today than it did then."

"Yes, of course," Larina said. "I was really thinking how fortunate it was that your grandfather in his wide search was able to buy so many ancient treasures which would otherwise have been lost, or perhaps deliberately destroyed by those who did not understand them."

There was a cynical smile on Wynstan's lips as he said:

"We appreciate them, and there are a number of us amongst whom the house and grounds must be divided."

He realised as he spoke that Larina was not listening, but following the train of her own thoughts.

"I have always longed to own a piece of Greek sculpture," she said. "Once I saw a marble foot in a shop window in London which I was certain was Greek, but it was too expensive and I could not afford it."

"Perhaps we can find you something while you are here," Wynstan replied. "In the obscure villages and in the poorer parts of Naples there are often treasures of which their owners have no idea of their value."

For a moment he thought Larina's eyes lit up. Then she said in a tone he did not understand:

"It is too . . . late now!"

They had talked after dinner until it was nearly midnight, and only the striking of the clock made Larina realise that perhaps she was being selfish.

"You must be tired," she said in consternation. "You have been travelling for days to come here and I should have suggested that we retire early."

Wynstan did not reply. He was tired not so much from the travelling as from the two nights he had spent in Paris.

He had in fact been feeling rather guilty after meeting Larina that he had been delayed by his own desire for enjoyment and therefore she had been alone in the Villa except for the servants.

She did not appear to have minded, but he could imagine that most women of his acquaintance would have been exceedingly annoyed at such cavalier treatment, even if they had not actually been frightened.

But Larina, he thought, seemed already a part of the Villa.

"Do you think that Elvin will arrive today?" she asked.

"He might," Wynstan answered cautiously. "Are you so impatient to see him?"

"Yes, I must see him . . . I must see him quickly!"

There was something in the way she spoke which made him look at her in surprise. Then leaving her breakfast unfinished she rose from the table and walked across the room to the window.

"Harvey must be right and she is having a baby," Wynstan told himself.

And yet as he looked at her slim figure

with its small waist silhouetted against the sunshine, it seemed highly improbable.

It was not only her figure which perplexed him; there was something in her eyes and in the expression on her face which made him feel it was impossible she could be anything but pure and innocent.

'I am a fool to be taken in by her!' Wynstan thought and he went on with his breakfast.

It was difficult to think that with his experience of women he could be deceived by someone as young and unsophisticated as Larina. Yet he knew, if he was honest, he would have staked a fortune that she was what she appeared to be.

There was something untouched and innocent about her which made him once again think of Aphrodite.

At the same time he had to face facts: she was certainly in a state of agitation because Elvin had not arrived as she had expected.

He could not know that Larina looking out onto the garden was telling herself there were only two days left.

Time had slipped by so quickly ever since Mr. Donaldson had called on her in London. The excitement of the journey abroad and the enchantment of the Villa when she arrived had made her almost forget that the sands of time were running out.

Today was the 13th. There was tomorrow and then . . .

She drew in her breath.

It was difficult to know how Sir John could have been so precise, but there had been something in the way he spoke and the gravity of his manner which told her he was utterly sure of his facts.

She felt her heart give a frightened leap.

Suppose it stopped now at this very moment when she was looking at the brilliance of the flowers and the butterflies hovering above them?

Then she told herself she had two days more besides the rest of today in which to enjoy all this beauty and she must not spoil it by fear.

With an effort she turned and went back to the table.

"If Elvin said he would come . . . I know he will keep his promise," she said, more as if she was speaking to herself than to Wynstan.

"What did he promise you?" he asked in a deliberately casual tone.

There was a moment's pause before Larina answered:

"That he would come to me . . . if I wanted him."

"And why do you want him so particularly?"

Wynstan did not look at her as he spoke but seemed intent on buttering a piece of bread.

There was a silence. Then at length Larina said:

"There is . . . something I have to tell . . . him."

"Would you not like to tell me? If it is a problem of any sort, I am sure I can solve it for you."

"No . . . no!" Larina cried sharply.

As Wynstan looked at her she added:

"Only Elvin will . . . understand. That is why I am so . . . anxious to see him."

Wynstan thought there was no point in pressing her at the moment.

Perhaps he might do so, but somehow it seemed unkind.

She seemed so young, such a child in some ways, that he could not bully her as Harvey would have done. Instead he felt certain that sooner or later he could charm her into telling him her secret.

"I was wondering whether you would like to come down to the jetty with me and see my motor-boat," he said in a different tone of voice.

"A motor-boat?" Larina exclaimed. "I

have never seen one!"

"They do exist!" Wynstan said with a smile, "and this is a boat I had specially made for me."

He saw she was interested and went on:

"I was friends with Captain William Newman, who two years ago crossed the Atlantic from West to East in a boat which had the unusual name of *'Abiel, Abbot Low'.*"

"I have never heard of him," Larina said.

"Perhaps the Americans were more excited about his achievement than the English," Wynstan said. "But it certainly made history since the boat was powered by a paraffin engine of a mere 12 h.p.!"

"And you have a boat like it?" Larina enquired.

"Not so big," he replied. "In fact mine is much smaller. Shall we go and look at it?"

"Oh, yes, I would love that! Will you wait while I get my hat?"

"Of course," he replied.

She ran from the room eagerly.

He looked after her with a puzzled expression in his eyes.

He supposed it was because he had had so little to do with young women that he found it difficult to understand her.

All his love-affairs had been with mature, sophisticated, social personalities who had enormous confidence in themselves and their attractions.

He knew that Larina was unsure of herself, and he found the way that she looked at him to see if she had said or done anything wrong was very appealing. She was very young!

And yet, their conversation last night had told him that she not only read a great deal but she also had a good mind.

He might have expected a banal, brainless conversation with a girl who was so young, or else a flirtatious coquettishness just because he was a man and she was a woman.

But Larina's mind, he found, was focused not on him, except in so far as he could instruct her, but on the mythology of which they talked and the gods and goddesses who seemed so much more real to her than human beings.

And yet, as she came running back to him, now holding a large straw hat in her hand, she had the excited eyes of a child being taken for a special treat.

Wynstan led the way through the garden and down the narrow steps which his grandfather had made in the cliff.

As they descended Larina could see below them a small rocky bay with an artificial breakwater and a jetty.

Tied up beside it was the motor-boat!

It was smaller than she had expected, feeling that anything to do with a motor must be large, and when they reached it Wynstan looked at it appreciatively.

It had a long, pointed bow she noticed, which she felt must contain the engine.

She could see the place where the driver stood in the centre of the boat and behind it was a small cabin which Wynstan showed her contained a table with two cushioned benches on either side of it which were large enough, if necessary, to turn into sleeping-bunks.

"This is a 'Napier Minor', if you are interested," he said, "and the firm which makes them confidently believes that it will win the first cross-channel race which will take place this year."

"It looks almost too small to cross the Channel."

"It is easy to handle."

"Will you drive it yourself?" she asked in surprise.

"I have every intention of doing so," he replied. "I like to ride my own race-horses, drive my own motor-cars and be the engine-driver of my own train!"

Larina laughed.

"I believe every small boy wants to be a train-driver!"

She did not realise that the Vanderfelds did in fact own a private train and that Wynstan often drove it.

Because he realised that once again he had made a slip of the tongue, he drew her attention to the boat, showing her it was made of seasoned cypress on white oak timbers.

"And it has a paraffin engine?" she asked hoping she was saying the right thing.

"Just like the one that crossed the Atlantic."

"Can we go to sea in it?"

"That is exactly what I was going to suggest," Wynstan replied. "Where would you like to go? Pompeii?"

The colour rose in her cheeks with excitement.

"Could we really do that?"

"There is no reason why not," he answered, "and it would be far quicker than making the journey by road."

He smiled as he added:

"I have a feeling that like all tourists you are determined to see Pompeii before you leave Italy, and so we might as well combine business with pleasure."

"I should have thought that driving the boat and seeing Pompeii were both pleasure!" Larina replied.

"I have to try her out before I pay the bill."

"Papa always said it was stupid to pay for anything unless one had made absolutely certain it was exactly what one had ordered."

"Your father was obviously very sensible," Wynstan approved.

He had taken his place at the wheel of the boat having started up the engine and cast off the ropes which tied it to the jetty.

Larina stood beside him as slowly he began to ease the vessel into the centre of the small bay and through the opening in the breakwater.

"This is exciting — very exciting!" Larina cried. "I never thought I would travel in a motor-boat! How fast can we go?"

She thought as she spoke that this was another thing of which her father would have disapproved because it meant speed.

She was sure he would have been quite content to row a little way from the cliffs and row back again, but instead they were out in the open sea and Larina could see the Gulf of Naples from a new angle.

The white houses, the cliff hamlets, the towers of the Churches, the vine-covered hills were an enchantment it was impossible to put into words.

Then there was Mt. Vesuvius dominating the horizon, somehow sinister even though it was bathed in sunshine.

There was a small plume of smoke rising from its cone and as she looked at it apprehensively Wynstan, as if he read her thoughts, asked:

"Are you nervous of encountering the same fearful catastrophe that took place in 79 A.D.?"

"I have read about it," Larina said, "but that is very different from seeing the place where it actually happened."

She was to think this again when an hour later they had entered the Port of Torre Annunziata and moored the motor-boat.

Then they had climbed up the cliff and taken an open carriage to Pompeii.

As they reached the entrance Wynstan waved away the guides who surged eagerly towards them.

"I came here so often when I was a boy," he said. "I want to see if I can remember everything about it. Enough at any rate, to keep you interested!"

"I do not want to miss anything!" Larina answered and Wynstan laughed.

They moved into the Forum where among the broken pillars he told her how Pompeii had been a prosperous industrial and trading centre.

It had sided with the Italic towns against the Romans and withstood a siege of nine years. But after the Pompeians had opened their gates because they could no longer go on fighting, a colony of Roman veterans had arrived in the town and it had become increasingly Romanized.

"You said it was industrial," Larina said. "What did they make?"

"It sounds amusing today," Wynstan replied, "but one particular export of the Pompeians was a popular brand of fish-sauce. Their wine trade was very important, and later of course like Herculaneum it became a resort for rich Romans."

They walked on, looking at the Temples near the Forum, at the *Building of Eumachia* who had been a priestess, and came to the Gladiators' Barracks.

"In these barracks," Wynstan said, "they found evidence of sixty-three people who had lost their lives there. One was a woman whose rich jewellery suggested that she was there on a visit to her Gladiator lover!"

"It must have been very frightening!" Larina said in a low voice.

"The earth tremors had been taking place for some time," Wynstan went on, "then on August 22nd they ceased. The sky was blue and cloudless but the air had a strange fore-boding silence."

Larina shivered.

There was something eerie in thinking of the people going about their ordinary business and not realising what was going to happen to them.

"The morning of the 24th was very hot," Wynstan continued, "the sky was clear and everyone's fears had subsided."

He looked round the Amphitheatre, which could hold twenty thousand spectators, to which they had walked while he was talking.

"Everyone was preparing for luncheon when a severe earth-tremor was followed by what seemed like a terrific clap of thunder."

He looked up.

"Everyone stopped what they were doing and turned to look at Vesuvius. The top of the mountain had literally burst open and was pouring forth a glowing fire."

Larina looked apprehensively at the thin column of smoke rising against the sky.

Wynstan's story was so dramatic that she almost felt it might change into fire at any moment.

"A huge mushroom-shaped cloud formed," he went on. "Then there was a series of explosions which hurled huge boulders high into the sky."

He paused before he continued:

"Suddenly it began to rain and mixed with the rain were cinders, pumicestones, lumps of large rock and dust which quickly turned to mud. The birds fell to the earth. In a matter of minutes the sun was obscured and the bright day had turned into the blackest night."

He looked out onto the Gulf.

"The sea was in a turmoil alternately retreating then flooding in with huge waves which pounded against the coast."

"What did the people do?" Larina enquired.

"I imagine they must have begun to run screaming from the town. There were twenty thousand of them, but more than two thousand are known to have lost their lives, under the hail of pumicestone, mud, cinders and ashes, which buried the town with such astounding rapidity."

"I cannot bear to think the people had no time to escape," Larina cried.

"I imagine that a great many more died than the archaeologists actually found inside Pompeii," Wynstan replied.

"Perhaps it was a quick way to . . . die," she said in a low voice. "After the first moments of terror they could have known . . .

nothing about it."

"I think it is a horrible way to die!" Wynstan said firmly. "When my time comes I want, like the Greeks, to die in the sun."

"That is what I want too."

There was something almost violent in her tone of voice which made him look at her sharply.

"You funny little thing! It has really upset you," he said in a kind voice. "I thought you liked excavating the past."

"It is . . . different when it concerns buildings, Temples, the statues of gods who are . . . immortal," Larina answered. "But these were ordinary people and they were not expecting death. So it seems somehow horribly intrusive to stare with curiosity at where they died."

"When one dies, can it matter where or how?" Wynstan asked.

"I do not . . . know," Larina replied. "But it is . . . frightening to think of them . . . screaming and fighting to . . . live!"

There was such genuine horror in her voice and in the expression in her eyes, that Wynstan put his arm through hers and said:

"Let us be more cheerful. It all happened a long time ago and neither you nor I are going to die for a very long time. Come and look at the Temple of Jupiter, and tell me if you can imagine it filled with spectators for the shows which were held there before the Amphitheatre was built."

He knew she made an effort to answer him as she replied:

"From what I have read about the Roman shows I should not have thought they were very suitable for a Temple!"

Wynstan laughed.

"You are right! But the Romans were a very practical people with little imagination and they developed a religion which corresponded with their needs."

"I tried . . . when I was journeying here," Larina said, "to think about the Romans. Instead I found myself so much more concerned with the Greeks."

'And one in particular,' she added secretly to herself, 'called Apollo.'

"I always find myself doing the same thing," Wynstan agreed. "The Romans felt no mystic necessity to love and worship the superhuman powers of the gods as they conceived them. At the same time Jupiter did have a certain majesty about him."

"I think he was cruel!" Larina argued. "His function was to warn men, to punish them, and for this purpose he possessed three thunder-bolts!"

"The Romans were a hard-fighting, cruel

people," Wynstan replied. "Jupiter was a warrior-god and he expected to be obeyed."

Larina did not answer him. They moved away from the Temple of Jupiter and wandered down the narrow streets, which had once teemed with people but now contained only the empty shells of their houses.

They saw the House of the Lyre Player, then began to wend their way gradually towards the exit.

"I am thinking of what you said about the Romans being cruel," Larina said. "I think the reason was that they did not worship beauty and their goddesses were not like those of Greece."

"That is true!" Wynstan agreed. "And they were cruel even to their Vestal Virgins. They took vows of absolute chastity but those who broke them were punished by being whipped to death."

"Oh, no!" Larina exclaimed involuntarily.

"Later this was modified," he went on. "They were whipped and then walled-up alive in a tomb which was sealed off with a few provisions deposited in it."

"No wonder people were afraid of the Romans."

"You need not worry about the Vestal Virgins too much," Wynstan smiled.

"During the course of eleven centuries only twenty broke their vows and suffered such punishment. But if a Vestal let the sacred fire go out she was whipped!"

"Let us talk instead about beautiful gods of the Greeks," Larina begged, "who Homer said 'tasted a happiness which lasted as long as their eternal lives'."

"One day you must obviously visit Greece."

Wynstan saw a strange expression come over Larina's face as he spoke and did not understand it.

He was wondering if she was thinking that she could not afford the journey, but somehow he sensed it was something more than that.

She did not answer and he did not want to question her.

They drove back to Torre Annunziata, but instead of getting into the boat Wynstan led Larina to a small restaurant at the side of the Quay.

There were tables outside in the sunshine and waiters hurried to attend to them as soon as they sat down.

"What would you like to eat?" he asked.

"Please order for me," Larina begged.

He chose *antipasto* of smoked ham with fresh figs to start with. After that they had

Zuppa di pesce the famous fish-soup of Southern Italy which he told Larina was a kind of *bouillabaisse* with differing ingredients from season to season.

Afterwards there was *Abbacchio al torno* — a typical Roman dish of suckling lamb seasoned with rosemary and garlic and roasted in the oven.

"I cannot eat any more!" Larina protested when she was begged to try other special Neapolitan delicacies.

But the waiter insisted that she finish her meal with a peeled peach in a glass of white wine, and she was not allowed to refuse the coffee because Wynstan told her that the coffee of Naples was the best in the world!

They drank a local wine, but Larina was disappointed to hear it was not *Vesuvino* which was grown on the slopes of Vesuvius.

"I am afraid that has deteriorated with time," Wynstan explained, "like *Falerno* which is still produced in the Phlegragan Fields. It was much praised in antiquity but I have come to believe that the classic taste was different from mine!"

He filled her glass as he said:

"This is *Epomea* which comes from the Isle of Ischia."

It was, Larina thought, delicious. Bright yellow in colour, it seemed to have captured some of the sunshine all around them.

They sat talking for a long time after their luncheon was finished until they finally got back into the motor-boat and started for home.

"Tomorrow I will take you to Ischia," Wynstan said. "It is one of my favourite islands, and of course another day we must visit Capri."

"That would be lovely!" Larina answered.

At the same time she wondered if she would ever see Capri.

She had the feeling that she was on an express train and it was going faster and faster but there was nothing she could do to stop it.

"I must not think of what lies ahead," she told herself. "I must live every moment, every second. I must cram everything into what time is left to me."

She knew she was growing more and more afraid and when she returned to the Villa and found that Elvin had not arrived she felt a moment of panic and had to fight for self-control.

Because Wynstan had been so kind to her Larina considered the idea of telling him the truth. Then she knew it was impossible to speak of her death to anyone except Elvin.

No-one else would understand. Wynstan would commiserate with her. He might also say it was impossible and try to give her false hope, and that would be even worse.

She would rather face the truth and be prepared.

When she had gone to bed last night she had prayed for a long time, not that she might live, but that she might be brave.

"No-one who is a Christian should be afraid of dying," she told herself severely.

But it was hard to practice what she knew was logical when death was coming nearer and nearer.

Everything that had ever frightened her about death, like the head of a skeleton, the trappings of a funeral, the dark veils and crêpe bands with which mourners paraded their grief seemed to flutter beside her as if they were birds of ill-omen.

Then she told herself there would be no-one to mourn her and no-one to assume black in her memory.

Perhaps she would die in the sun as Wynstan wished to do, and she knew that would be the perfect way for her 'spirit to take wings'.

And if Elvin was beside her, holding her hand, she would not be afraid.

Then she would imagine she was flying

away into the blue of the sky and into the arms of Apollo who would hold her close. When there was no longer any life, there would be no fear either.

"What are you thinking about?" Wynstan asked suddenly, breaking in on her thoughts.

They were sitting outside the Villa on the terrace where the servants had brought them cool drinks and the fragrance of the flowers was almost overwhelming.

"I was thinking . . . of death!" Larina said without choosing her words.

"Pompeii has upset you," he said. "Forget about it. Tomorrow you will see the loveliness of Ischia. It too has a volcanic mountain, but it has never been known to erupt. Instead it has luxuriant vineyards, olive groves, pine forests and the chestnut trees are very beautiful. We will sit and drink the island's delicious wine and talk about life."

"That would be . . . lovely!" Larina said.

But he felt there was still a shadow in her grey eyes. Bending towards her he said in a voice which women always found irresistible:

"Will you not tell me what worries you?"

Larina shook her head.

"I am waiting for . . . Elvin."

"Supposing, after all, Elvin cannot come?"

He saw that she was startled and went on choosing his words with care:

"He may have been taken ill on the journey. He may have found it too much for him. It is a long way for him to travel."

"Yes, of course, I thought of that. But Mr. Donaldson said he had had a cable from him saying he would definitely meet me here."

"And the idea pleased you?"

"It was what I wanted more than anything else in the world — to be with Elvin at this moment."

"Why particularly at this moment?"

Larina did not answer and after a moment Wynstan said:

"I asked you a question, Larina. Why particularly at this moment?"

There was a pause, then she said:

"Did I say that? I was thinking of his being here . . . of our being together. That is what I meant."

Wynstan had the feeling she was not telling him the truth.

Suddenly Larina said in a voice that was tense and agitated:

"He must come! If anything had prevented him he would have sent a cable! We should have heard by now! Surely he will arrive tomorrow?"

There was a note of tension, of despair in her voice and Wynstan looked at her in a puzzled manner.

Even if she were having Elvin's child, why should there be so much urgency for her to see him?

If she meant him to marry her, there was plenty of time before there was any chance of the child being born.

And if it was not a baby which was troubling her, then what could it be?

Because he could see she was not far from tears he said soothingly:

"Perhaps we shall have news of Elvin tomorrow, but there is nothing we can do just now."

"No, of course not," Larina said with an effort. "I am being foolish! It is just that I was . . . so looking forward to seeing him . . . I felt you would understand."

Wynstan told himself he did not understand, but there was no point at the moment in saying so.

He felt he was being rather dilatory in not pressing Larina further, in not finding out about Elvin's letters, and most of all about what she wished to tell his brother.

But he found it difficult deliberately to

sweep away the happiness in her face and to see it replaced by an expression to which he could not put a name, but which seemed to him to be something near terror.

As he talked quietly to her of other things, gradually he realised that Larina had recovered her composure, and when they both went to change for dinner she was laughing.

Dinner was once again a superb meal. They had finished it and moved into the Drawing-Room where Wynstan began to look for some photographs to show Larina of what the Villa had looked like before his grandfather started to rebuild it.

As he was searching for them there was suddenly the sound outside of a carriage and horses.

Wynstan went to the window which overlooked the front of the house and saw a large, private brougham had drawn up at the front door. Out of it were getting several people, among them a woman in an evening-gown.

"Who is it?" Larina asked. "Could it be Elvin?"

"No," Wynstan replied. "It is visitors. I do not think they should find you here. It would be difficult to explain why you have no Chaperon."

Larina looked at him and said quickly:

"Yes, you are right! I will go upstairs."

As she spoke Wynstan realised that the guests, whoever they might be, had already been let into the house by the servants.

He had given no instructions to turn callers away and the Italians, who were always hospitable, would show anyone who arrived into the Drawing-Room.

"You will be seen," he said to Larina. "Go by the garden — I will get rid of them quickly!"

Without a word Larina ran across the room and out of the open window into the garden.

The stars had come out while they were talking, the moon was climbing up the sky, and it was not dark.

She had only to walk along the terrace to find another door into the Villa, but she stopped and hesitated.

Then she started up the path which climbed to the Temple.

When she was free of the lights of the house she stopped again to move from the steps, to amongst the azaleas. She sat down on the ground so that the shrubs reached above her head.

Through the flowers she could see the lights pouring from the windows of the Drawing-Room onto the terrace and she wondered if she would catch a glimpse of Wynstan's guests.

She was curious — very curious!

Wynstan waiting in the Drawing-Room heard voices coming down the corridor. Then the first person to enter the room was the Contessa Spinello whom he had known in Rome and had also met in Monte Carlo the previous year.

She was dark, vivacious, very lovely, and with diamonds glittering round her neck and in her ears she seemed to sparkle as she ran across the room towards him and raised her face to his.

"Wynstan — it is true!" she cried in her fascinating broken English. "I heard you had arrived, but I did not believe it!"

"It is delightful to see you, Nicole," Wynstan answered, "but who told you I was here?"

"Do you not suppose that the whole of Sorrento is talking about the Vanderfelds having opened their Villa again after so many years? And that a Vanderfeld 'molto bello' had arrived. Who could that be but you?"

"Who indeed?" Wynstan replied with an amused smile.

He held out his hand to her brother who

182

with two other men had followed the Contessa into the room.

"How are you, Antonio?" he asked. "It is nice to see you again."

"I did not believe it, but I hoped you were here," Antonio answered. "When we bought a Villa on the other side of Sorrento three years ago, we were told that the Vanderfelds never visited such an unfashionable neighbourhood!"

"It must be fashionable if you are living here!" Wynstan said.

"Did I not tell you that he always says the right thing?" the Contessa enquired of the two other men who were waiting to be introduced, and who were both Italians.

Wynstan shook hands with them, then the Contessa said:

"You must come and visit us immediately, Wynstan. What about dinner tomorrow? Chuck is arriving from Rome — you remember Chuck? You were at college with him."

"Chuck Kennedy? Of course I remember," Wynstan agreed. "But I will have to let you know about dinner."

"If not tomorrow — the next night," the Contessa insisted. "I will not take no for an answer! I want you to see our delightful Villa, although naturally it does not compare with yours!"

"How is your motor-boat, Antonio?" Wynstan enquired. "I have just had my new 'Napier Minor' delivered."

"What is it like?" Antonio enquired.

"I tried it out today and it seemed excellent!" Wynstan replied.

"Now stop talking about motor-boats, both of you," the Contessa ordered, "and talk about me! Wynstan is the love of my life and I cannot bear his predilection for mechanical objects!"

"Shall I tell you you are looking more beautiful than ever?" Wynstan enquired. "I expect that is what you really want to hear."

"But of course I do!" she smiled at him. "No-one can say such nice things as you, and even though they are insincere one believes them."

"Why should you doubt my sincerity?" Wynstan asked.

"Because there is a little twist to your lips, a look in your eyes, that belies everything you say," the Contessa replied. "Nevertheless I believe what I want to believe — it makes me happy!"

"That is a very good philosophy," one of the Italians remarked. "I wish I could do the same."

"Try it," the Contessa replied.

She flashed a flirtatious glance over her shoulder and walked through the open window out onto the terrace.

"Oh—your garden!" she exclaimed. "We have a dozen gardeners struggling to create one for our Villa, but it will never look like this!"

Wynstan followed her out and now Larina could see them standing in the light from the room behind them.

She could see the fashionable outline of the woman's gown, the jewels sparkling round her neck and on her wrists and it was impossible not to notice the way she turned her face enticingly towards Wynstan's.

Then the Contessa glanced back to see that her brother and his friends had not followed her, and slipping her arm through Wynstan's she drew him away from the open window along the terrace and nearer to where Larina was hiding.

"I have missed you, Wynstan," she said in a soft tone. "I had thought you might have come to Rome this winter. As you did not, I have been praying we would meet in Monte Carlo, but again you disappointed me!"

"You must forgive me," Wynstan said, "but I have been on a visit to India and actually arrived back in America only a week or so ago."

"Then you came here. Why?"

"I had a reason," Wynstan replied evasively, "and now the Villa has been opened up again I am sorry I have not been here before."

"But you will come again — and anyway, you are here now!" the Contessa answered. "We must see a lot of each other."

"Your husband is with you?" Wynstan enquired.

"He is in Florence," the Contessa replied. "That is what makes it so perfect!"

She lifted her face to Wynstan's and Larina watching knew that she expected him to kiss her.

She was sitting amongst the azaleas spellbound by what was happening below her.

She had not imagined that two people could look so attractive, Wynstan with his broad shoulders and narrow hips like the god she thought he resembled, and the Contessa with her raven-black hair which grew in a widow's peak on her oval forehead.

Her dark eyes seemed to flash in the darkness and Larina saw she had long, pointed fingers as she placed them on Wynstan's shoulder and pressed herself against him

He glanced towards the Drawing-Room window.

"We must go back."

"Why?" the Contessa asked. "Antonio knows I want to be with you. I love you, Wynstan — I have never forgotten the happiness we found together! Have you?"

"No, of course not."

"You are tired of me," the Contessa said. "Is there someone else? But that is a stupid question!"

She made a sound of exasperation and went on:

"There is always somebody else where you are concerned. Always, always! And yet I believed you could come back to me because our love must have meant as much to you as it did to me."

"You are very beautiful and very attractive," Wynstan said, "but, Nicole, you cannot expect me to believe there have not been a dozen men to take my place."

"Dozens!" the Contessa said lightly, "but none of them were you — none of them had that power to excite me in the way you did."

"You flatter me!" Wynstan said and there was a note of laughter in his voice.

Then as if she was tired of talking the Contessa put her arms round his neck and drew his head down to hers.

He kissed her. It was a long kiss.

Then firmly, with his arm around her shoulders, Wynstan drew her back towards the Drawing-Room and in through the lighted window.

Larina realised she was holding her breath.

She had never before seen two people kissing each other passionately. She had never seen a man holding a woman so that they were locked together by love.

It gave her a strange feeling within her breast — a feeling she did not understand.

Yet there had been something in the angle of Wynstan's head, the manner his lips had met the Contessa's, the closeness of their bodies against each other, which made her feel she watched something momentous taking place.

But the Contessa was married!

Then Larina told herself this was the way fashionable people behaved. She had read about it, she had heard people talk of the King's flirtations and the behaviour of the 'Marlborough House Set'.

But reading and listening were very different from seeing, and in particular from watching Wynstan, with whom she had spent the day, kiss somebody so lovely and attractive as the woman who had been with him on the terrace.

It was no concern of hers!

"No-one will ever kiss me like that!" Larina whispered and it was a cry of despair.

Chapter Six

Larina waited a moment or two and then rose from amongst the azaleas to step down the path.

Running across the terrace she entered the Villa by a garden door which led her into a passage off the Hall.

Here there was another staircase leading to the first floor. She hurried up it and into her bed-room, and closed the door.

For the first time since she had been at the Villa she did not pull back the curtains to look out over the sea at the lights of Naples twinkling in the distance or those which glowed round the bay wherever there was a fishing-village or a house.

Instead she undressed and got into bed.

Every night since she had come to the Villa she had been thrilled by the comfort and luxury of her bed-room.

It not only had a magnificent view from the balcony from where she could look out in the day-time, but it also was far more luxurious than anything she had ever known in her life before.

There was a bathroom adjoining where

the bath was sunk in the floor as had been the custom in Roman times.

It was very American, she knew, to have a bathroom attached to every main bed-room in the house and when she sat in her marble bath with its colourful tiles copied from those which must have decorated the original Villa, she felt herself carried back in time.

She would pretend she was the wife of a Roman Senator, or perhaps his daughter, and that waiting outside was all the pomp and glitter which had been characteristic of the Romans wherever they were.

But tonight all Larina wanted was to creep into bed and in the darkness tell herself that the sooner she went to sleep the better!

She wanted to see Wynstan again, she wanted desperately to go on talking to him, to be with him alone as they had been before the Italian beauty with her glittering diamonds had arrived.

Yet at the same time she could not bear to see him, knowing he had just kissed the lovely Nicole and he would be thinking of her.

She could not understand her own feelings; she only knew that the strange emotion in her breast, which she had felt as she had watched him kissing Nicole, had now become a vivid pain — a pain which was so intense that she wondered for a moment if she was on the point of dying.

Even as she thought of it she longed to run downstairs, throw herself into Wynstan's arms and ask him to hold her closely.

How could she make him understand that she needed his strength and she wanted him to give her courage?

Then she told herself he would only despise her for being a coward.

He had laughed at her today when she had been upset in Pompeii. He had not understood that to think of the Pompeians choking to death under the black pall of dust and pumicestone had made her afraid that was how she would feel when she came to die.

Suppose she had to endure the horror of choking, of suffocating as life left her body? Or feeling helpless, terror-struck, and having nowhere to turn for comfort?

How could she tell Wynstan of such things? She felt that close proximity with someone who was about to die would bore, if it did not disgust him.

Elvin was different. Elvin had lived so long with the thought of death that he would understand. He would be able to make her believe that it did not matter: that it was only the release of the spirit from the body and one was much happier once one was free.

"I want to believe . . . I want to believe!" Larina whispered in the darkness.

Then she found it difficult to keep her mind on death when all she could see was Wynstan kissing Nicole, his arms enfolding her, his head bent to hers.

"Perhaps I could ask Wynstan to kiss me once before I die," Larina said to herself and wondered if he would be shocked as well as surprised.

She had always believed that a woman did not ask a man to kiss her, and yet Nicole had put her arms around his neck and drawn his lips down to hers.

What had she felt? Had it been a sort of rapture, Larina wondered, which she herself had never experienced?

She had been in bed a long time when she heard voices outside and the sound of a carriage driving away.

They had gone! It was not very late and perhaps Wynstan would be expecting her to return to the Drawing-Room.

She could not bear to see him, not tonight with his lips still warm from Nicole's.

She found herself listening. The Villa was

very quiet. She wondered where Wynstan was; whether perhaps he had left with his friends and gone to spend the rest of the evening with them.

Then as she lay there tense, her mind chaotic with feelings she did not understand but which were nevertheless very intense, she heard him coming along the passage.

His room was on the other side of the house and therefore he must be coming to her.

She held her breath.

There was a tap on the door.

"Who is . . . it?" she asked, although she knew the answer.

"Are you all right, Larina?"

"Yes . . . quite!"

"Then sleep well! Good-night!"

"Good . . . night!"

Her voice was hardly loud enough for him to hear it. Then as she heard his footsteps going back towards his own room she started to cry.

She had not cried since her mother died. She had not shed a tear since she had known that she too must die.

Now she cried helplessly and desperately for herself, because her life was nearly at an end and because she would never know love.

She cried until her pillow was wet with tears and she felt in the darkness that everyone had forsaken her: Elvin, Wynstan and . . . Apollo.

Wynstan had been quite sure that Larina would go to her bed-room as she had said she would.

At the same time he did not wish to linger in the garden with Nicole.

They had enjoyed a wild, tempestuous, fiery affair in Rome the previous year. But before he left he had realised that the flames were dying down and as usual he was growing bored and a little impatient.

He could never explain to himself why a woman who had first seemed so desirable should suddenly begin to pall.

The little mannerisms which at first he had found fascinating became irritants; he knew what she was going to say before she said it. As always in his *affaires de coeur* he ceased to be the hunter and became the hunted.

Nicole had been no exception.

The moment she felt he was cooling off she pursued him relentlessly, and he found it more and more difficult to escape from her demands, to avoid finding himself isolated with her even in the midst of the gay, over-hospitable Roman society.

If he accepted an invitation to other friends, Nicole always managed to be there, and somehow it was inevitable, because she arranged it, that he had to take her home.

Which meant there was no escape from her clinging arms and her demanding lips.

The Count, who had interests of his own, was seldom at home. He had properties in the north of Italy where he preferred to spend most of his time.

Nicole made it very clear that the only tie which kept them together was the fact that they were Catholics and divorce was impossible.

The last person Wynstan had expected to see, or indeed wanted to see in Sorrento, was Nicole, and he had no intention of accepting her pressing invitations or of inviting her to the Villa.

That was not to ensure that she would not invite herself! He thought irritably there was nothing more tiresome than a woman who would not admit that a light-hearted affair was finished and there was no chance of resuscitating it.

Wynstan sighed as he realised he would have to be firm and make it very clear that he had no intention of being any longer at her beck and call.

There had been a few occasions in the past when he was forced to be ruthless, but usually the women he had loved became friends and he liked the sort of friendship which could mellow with the years into something very precious.

But he knew that Nicole would never come into that category, and he told himself that when he wrote her a note tomorrow saying that he could not accept her invitation to dinner, he would make her understand, once and for all, that it was the end of their association.

His thoughts sent him to Larina.

It had not been polite to ask her to leave so that she should not meet his friends, but he knew that Nicole would address him by his correct name, which would involve him in explanations that he had no wish to make at the moment.

Always at the back of his mind was Harvey's contention that Larina was out for money.

There was no doubt that she was desperate to see Elvin, and whether it was to make him marry her or to provide for her, it would be a mistake to let her know exactly how much Elvin was worth.

It seemed impossible to think of Larina as being concerned about money.

Yet from what she had told him in the course of their conversations Wynstan was aware that she and her mother had been living in poor circumstances.

She had explained that they were in Dr. Heinrich's Sanatorium, which was extremely expensive, only because he had taken them on special terms because her father had been a Doctor.

Wynstan knew London well enough to know that Eaton Terrace was a cheap neighbourhood from a residential point of view.

At the same time he had no wish to hurt Larina and he felt she might have felt insulted at being pushed out into the garden and having to go upstairs to sit in her bed-room while he entertained his friends.

When they had left he thought perhaps she might have gone to the Temple.

The moonlight was silver on the garden as Wynstan walked up the stone paths that were turned to a translucent grey.

The moon not only illuminated the world with a strange mystic beauty, but appeared to bring with it a feeling of quiet and of stillness which Wynstan felt had a message for him.

It was the same stillness he had felt the moment after Elvin had died.

It had been in the morning and he had been with his brother alone.

He had gone in to speak to Elvin. Then when he had risen to leave him, Elvin had put out his thin hand.

"Stay with me, Wynstan."

"Of course."

Wynstan sat down beside him on the side of his bed.

"I want you to be with me. You have always understood."

"I have always tried to," Wynstan answered.

The words he was saying meant nothing. He had known as he took Elvin's cold hand that he was dying and there was nothing he could do about it.

He made no attempt to call anyone. The nurses were only just outside, the Doctor could be reached in a few minutes. But he knew with a perception that was always there where Elvin was concerned that it was a waste of time.

They were together with a closeness they had known ever since they were children and as Elvin's fingers tightened on his hand, Wynstan knew that this was the end.

Elvin's eyes were closed. Then suddenly he opened them and there was a light in them.

"It is . . . wonderful . . . to be . . . free!" he said. "Tell . . ."

His voice died away, his eyes closed and his fingers relaxed.

Wynstan sat very still.

For a moment it seemed to him there was something moving in the room almost like a flutter of wings. Then there was only the stillness and a silence so absolute that he thought he could hear his own heart beating.

He had not been able to speak of those last moments with Elvin to anyone, not even to his mother.

He had sat for a long time on the bed thinking of Elvin, but knowing he was no longer there and the body he had left behind was unimportant.

It was with a superhuman effort, because he knew he had to face the world again, that he had risen to tell the nurses that their patient no longer had any need of their services.

Then he had gone out of the house to walk alone in Central Park.

He forced himself when he returned not to grieve for Elvin. No-one who loved him could want him to go on living with his illness destroying him, making every breath he drew difficult and laboured.

And Wynstan knew too although he could never speak of it to anyone, that Elvin was not dead.

Now as he reached the Temple Wynstan thought how Elvin would have loved the beauty of the moonlight and the statue of Aphrodite.

She seemed almost to be alive as she stood there on her pedestal with the lilies at her feet and her head turned to look out over the sea below.

Wynstan found himself remembering how when he had come up to the Temple on his arrival, Larina had been standing in much the same pose, her head turned away from him, her hair vivid with tongues of fire from the setting sun.

He remembered that strange feeling when for one second he had thought she must be Aphrodite herself.

He thought now it was the impression of slim, untouched virginity about both Larina and Aphrodite which made them seem alike.

He thought too, that when he had stared at the statue as a boy he had always been sure that the goddess had grey eyes, a small straight nose, and curved lips that were not sensuous but sensitive.

"The goddess of love!" Wynstan said aloud, then abruptly he turned and went back to the Villa.

He had gone to the Drawing-Room,

hoping that perhaps Larina had come downstairs once she heard his friends leaving, but the room was empty!

So he went to her bed-room to make quite certain that she was there and safely in bed.

He thought her voice trembled when she answered him. Then he told himself that doubtless she had been half-asleep and he had woken her.

As he walked to his own room, Wynstan wondered, as he had wondered all day, what was the secret that Larina was hiding which she would convey only to Elvin.

Because she felt she had wasted so much of her precious time in going to bed early and in tears Larina rose very early.

The dawn was only just breaking as she drew back the curtains of her bed-room and she decided that she must see it from the Temple perhaps for the last time.

Tomorrow was the day she would die and she had no way of knowing whether it would be early in the morning or late in the evening and therefore she was determined that today must not be wasted.

She looked at herself in the mirror and realised she must wash away the traces of the tears she had shed the night before, in case Wynstan should question her.

In the morning light she faced the fact frankly that some of her unhappiness had been due to the fact that she had seen him kissing the Italian and she thought how humiliating it would be if he ever guessed what had upset her.

"He is far more perceptive," she told herself, "than I imagined a man could ever be."

So often when they were talking he would be aware of what she was going to say almost before she said it, and when she could not put what she felt or thought into words he would do it for her. He never misunderstood what had been her intention.

As she finished dressing she felt herself longing with a physical yearning to see him again.

There was so little time left for her to be with him! Only today and perhaps part of tomorrow. Then she would be gone and he would go back to America and never think of her again.

Because she realised her tears the night before had left her pale with shadows under her eyes she chose the brightest of her summer gowns which she had bought at Peter Robinson.

It was a muslin of tiny pink and white stripes, trimmed round the neck and over the shoulders with white *broderie anglaise* which also edged the two frills of the skirt.

It made her look very young, like a rose which was not yet in bloom. But Larina had no time to spare on her reflection.

She swept her hair back from her forehead in the fashion which Charles Gibson sketched so attractively. Then she opened her bed-room door and tip-toed down the stairs so as not to wake Wynstan if he was still asleep.

She let herself out of the Villa and climbed to the Temple.

The dawn was just breaking as she reached it, and now Aphrodite's beauty was not the shimmering silver that Wynstan had seen the night before but warm, almost flesh-coloured, in the first glow of the sun.

Larina leant over the balustrade to see the sea slowly turning from grey to emerald, the sky from blue to crimson.

It was so lovely that she drew in her breath and felt for a moment as if she had wings and could fly out to greet the sun-god when he appeared over the horizon.

She found herself repeating the last words of a poem she had read, by Pindar.

"We are all shadows. But when the
    shining comes from the hands of
    God,

Then the heavenly light falls on man, and life is all sweetness."

"The heavenly light!" Larina repeated to herself and wanted to hold out her arms towards it, to feel it enfolding her as if it was in fact a man and she was in Apollo's arms.

Apollo's or Wynstan's?

The question came to her and she knew for the moment it was impossible to divide them. They were one and the same and she wanted their closeness.

Larina had nearly finished her breakfast when Wynstan joined her.

"Good-morning!" he smiled. "The servants told me you were up very early. You put me to shame!"

"You slept well?"

"If I need an excuse, I read until very late," he answered. "I found a book which I think will interest you, and I will tell you about it when we are at Ischia."

"We are going there for lunch?"

"That is what I planned," Wynstan answered, "but I thought as we are early this morning, we would take the boat straight there across the open bay instead of keeping under the shelter of the coast. You wanted to see how fast she would go, and it is something I want to know myself."

"That sounds exciting!" Larina exclaimed.

Wynstan turned to the servant.

"Has the mechanic seen to the motor-boat?"

"*Si, Signor,* he is down there now."

"Good!" Wynstan answered. "I want to talk to him."

He rose to his feet saying to Larina:

"Join me when you are ready. There is no hurry: I have one or two things I want to discuss with my mechanic."

Larina fetched her hat and when she was in her bed-room she wondered if they were going out to sea whether she would need a coat. Then she told herself it was already warm and looked like being a hot day.

She put on the big straw, having changed the ribbons from the green one which had encircled the crown yesterday to a pink one which matched the dress she was wearing.

"I expect the wind will blow it away if we go very fast," she told herself practically, "but I will wear it to go down to the Quay."

She knew it was becoming, and she had thought when she wore it yesterday as they walked around Pompeii there had been a look of unmistakable admiration in Wynstan's eyes.

Then she felt with a little drop of her heart that it was unlikely he would admire her since she was fair while the woman he had kissed last night was dark.

"I am sure fair men like dark women," she told herself despondently, then shook herself mentally.

'At least I will be alone with him all day today,' she thought. 'After that will it matter to me who he is with?'

Because she had no wish to waste any time she ran down the stairs and out into the garden.

The bees were already busy amongst the flowers, the butterflies seemed brighter than ever, as she started the descent down the cliff.

She could see Wynstan below her talking to the mechanic and the motor-boat gleaming white in the water.

As she reached them Wynstan turned to smile at her.

"Everything is ready," he said, "and now we must see what speed-records we can break!"

"Can we really break one?"

"We can try," Wynstan replied. "At the same time if we come back and say we have done a hundred miles per hour no-one will believe us!"

"I am sure that would be impossible!" Larina smiled.

They moved slowly out of the little harbour and Wynstan headed out to sea.

He stood at the wheel and Larina stood beside him resting her arms on the woodwork in front of her.

When they had gone a little way she took off her hat and bending down threw it into the cabin behind her.

"You must not get sun-burnt," Wynstan said.

"Why not?" she asked.

"Because women should be white-skinned," he answered, "like goddesses who are sculpted in marble."

"I do not believe I sun-burn easily," Larina answered. "And at the moment there is no sun."

That was true.

The sun which had risen so gloriously at dawn seemed to have disappeared.

Now the sky overhead was grey and there were some ominous-looking clouds to the north.

"They will go away," Larina told herself hopefully.

She could not bear to miss the sunshine today of all days.

They drove on and now Wynstan was increasing the speed until it seemed to Larina that they almost flew over the water.

Away from the shelter of the coast the sea was rough, far rougher than it had been yesterday. Now there was the slap of the waves against the bow which with their speed seemed almost to be lifted out of the water.

Larina looked back.

Now they were a long way from the shore and the mountains in the background were rising higher and still higher.

She could see Mt. Vesuvius very clearly, its small column of smoke like a ghost in the air above it.

She could see Naples and immediately behind them the small Isle of Capri.

On they went, until soon it was difficult to distinguish anything in the distance except the outline of the mountains.

There was something exhilarating in being surrounded only by sea and almost out of sight of human habitation.

Then suddenly there was a splutter from the engine and it stopped.

"Blast!" Wynstan ejaculated.

"What has happened?" Larina enquired.

Everything seemed suddenly very silent after the noise of the engine and the boat began to rock on the waves.

"I shall have to find out," Wynstan replied.

He took off his light summer coat and, as Larina had done, threw it behind him into the cabin.

Then he rolled up the sleeves of his shirt, and opened two doors low down on the floor so that he could look at the engine.

"Do you know what has gone wrong?" Larina asked.

"I can guess," he answered. "But it could be a number of things. I suppose, if I had been sensible, I would have brought the mechanic with us."

'That would have spoilt everything!' Larina thought.

She could not say so to Wynstan, but it was very exciting for her to be alone with a man!

It was something she had never experienced before and something which she knew she ought not to be doing now.

No well-brought-up young woman would have dreamt of going off in a motor-boat, of all modern inventions, without even knowing where she was being taken.

Larina was well aware it would have shocked not only her mother but certainly all the acquaintances they had known in the days when they lived in Sussex Gardens.

Larina could remember the ladies who had called on her mother and come to her 'at home' days, and also those who came to the house for the purpose of consulting her father.

The Dining-Room was always used as a waiting-room. Larina would sometimes peep in to see the fashionably dressed women, wearing sables and ostrich feathers in their hats, turning over the magazines which were laid on the table every morning by one of the maids.

Sometimes they left behind an expensive fragrance and when they went from the Dining-Room into her father's consulting room she would hear the rustle of their silk petticoats under their full skirts.

Yes, they would definitely be shocked at her behaviour, but as they would never know about it why should she even think of them?

Wynstan, who had been half-inside the lower-deck, pulled himself out to say:

"You will find some papers in a drawer in the cabin. Please bring them to me. There should be a plan of the boat somewhere amongst them."

Larina did as she was told.

When she had found the papers and was emerging from the cabin to hand them to Wynstan, she realised it was getting far rougher than it had been before.

Now the boat was rocking almost violently from side to side, and occasionally it pitched forward which made her stagger so that she had to hold on to something.

Wynstan sat on the floor studying the plans she had given him.

"Can I help?" she asked.

"Not unless you understand paraffin engines."

Larina looked back the way they had come.

Now it was impossible to see even the mountains.

A grey mist seemed to have descended over them and after looking at it for some time she realized it was rain.

A few seconds later she felt the first drops and heard them spatter on the foredeck. They also fell on the papers which Wynstan was studying.

"This is ridiculous!" he said angrily. "I thought I knew all about engines."

He picked up a tool and half-disappeared through the door. Only his legs remained outside and Larina knew he would get wet.

She was just wondering whether she should go and sit in the cabin, when a squall of rain so heavy it seemed almost torrential poured down on her so that in a few seconds she was soaked to the skin.

What was more the boat was rocking so dangerously from side to side that she felt frightened to move in case she should fall and hurt herself.

Thinking it was the only possible thing to do she sat down on the deck. The rain was beating on her so heavily that it was quite painful against her face and on her shoulders which were only covered with the fine muslin of her gown.

A long time later Wynstan pulled himself out of the engine-room.

"I cannot find it," he said in an exasperated tone. "I thought it must be the pistons but I have checked every one."

Larina looked at him helplessly through the rain.

"Why do you not sit in the cabin?" he asked.

"It is so rough I was afraid to move."

"I will help you."

"What is the point? I am wet now, I might as well get wetter!"

He smiled at her.

"Are you frightened?"

She shook her head.

"I am only thankful I do not feel seasick."

"Well, that is one blessing and we had better start counting them. It looks as if we are going to be here for a long time."

He collected some more tools and once again put his head under the floorboards.

Larina sat patiently.

The rain was now not so violent, but a strong wind made the sea even more tempestuous than it had been already.

The boat was thrown about on the waves and every so often one broke over the stern in a shower of spray.

It must have been two hours later that Wynstan stood up and steadying himself on the deck-rail, tried to start the engine.

For a moment there was nothing, then there was a splutter which quickly died.

It was, however, encouraging and Larina rose to stand beside him.

"Do you think you have found out what was wrong?" she asked.

"I hope so," he answered. "There was a wire that was broken. I have repaired it, but it may not hold."

He tried the engine again, and this time it ran for five or six seconds before once again it spluttered into silence.

Wynstan was back on the floor, then another ten minutes later he came out again.

This time the engine started and roared into life.

It seemed to Larina that they both held

their breath in suspense, but there was no splutter and it appeared to be running smoothly.

"You have done it! You have done it!" she cried.

Wynstan turned to smile at her.

She was standing very close to him.

As he looked down his smile deepened. She was soaked to the skin and her muslin gown clung to her so that she might in fact have been wearing nothing.

It revealed her small breasts and clung tightly over her hips to the ground.

The wind had blown her hair loose and it fell on either side of her cheeks nearly to her waist, framing her small face and her huge grey eyes.

"You look exactly like one of the Sirens who tempted Ulysses," Wynstan exclaimed.

Then he put his arms around her and kissed her.

For a moment Larina felt her lips cold against his, then something wild and ecstatic ran through her like forked lightning.

She knew that this was what she had longed for, this was what she wanted! She felt his lips were suddenly warm and at the same time hard and demanding.

It must have been only a moment that he held her against him and his mouth possessed hers, and yet it seemed to Larina as if the whole world was hers and the stars fell from the sky around her.

It was a wonder and a rapture that she had never believed possible. Then Wynstan released her and said in a voice that was somehow strange:

"I said that you were a Siren, Larina!"

He put both his hands on the wheel and very slowly turned the boat round.

She stood beside him without moving. It was impossible to do anything but cling to the fore-deck to steady herself, and feel as if her whole body had come alive.

It was the same feeling, she thought, that she had known when she had become part of the flowers and the water.

The same, and yet in many ways even more wonderful, more ecstatic.

"We shall have to go rather slowly," Wynstan said, "or it will break down again. I am afraid it is going to take us a long time to get home."

'It does not matter — nothing matters!' Larina wanted to say, but it was impossible for her to speak.

She could only look at Wynstan's profile as he stared ahead of them and feel that she was still quivering from the wonder of his lips.

He drove for a little way in silence, before he asked:

"What are you thinking?"

"I was thinking of a poem," Larina answered truthfully.

"Then it should be the lines written by Sophocles when he said: 'Many marvels there are, but none so marvellous as Man!'."

He gave a little laugh.

"That is me! Because I assure you it was very marvellous of me to have repaired this engine! If it gets us home safe and sound, it will be a miracle!"

"And if you had not mended it?" Larina asked.

"Then we might have been drifting for hours, even days, before we were picked up — unless we had swum back to the shore."

Larina gave a little laugh and looked at the distant coast which was still shrouded in mist.

"The only possible way of doing that would be to ride on the back of a dolphin!"

"Of course, if the gods behaved properly, they would send us a dolphin each!" he answered lightly.

Larina did not answer and after a moment he said:

"I am interested to hear of which poem

you were thinking."

"Yours is better!" she answered.

"I am waiting," Wynstan said.

Shyly, her voice low but just loud enough for him to hear it above the engine, she quoted the lines that seemed to have been in her mind since she came to the Villa.

"He who has won some new splendour
Rides on the air,
Borne upward on the wings of his human vigour."

Although this came from an ode to Apollo, asking his special blessing for those who had won victory in the Pythian games, it was particularly applicable to Wynstan.

No-one could have looked more strong and vigorous than he did at this moment, his soaked shirt revealing the breadth of his shoulders, the strength of his arms and the athletic lines of his body.

His wet trousers outlined his narrow hips and Larina knew without being told that he was tremendously strong and that in a fight his adversary would come off worst.

"If you are referring to me," Wynstan said with a smile, "you have omitted two rather important lines of the poem."

"What are they?" Larina asked.

"For a brief space the exultant of joy,
Until at last he falls to the earth,
Shattered by the beckoning doom!"

He laughed.

"In other words: 'Pride comes before a fall,' and that is something it is always wise to remember."

"Why should you fall?" Larina asked. "I am sure you never will."

"I hope you are right," he said. "But it is a mistake for one to become too conceited or to think oneself invincible."

"I have never been able to think that," Larina said, "but you are different. You would always get your own way, you would always be able to do the impossible and turn defeat into victory."

"Now again you are like the Sirens who sang to Ulysses. Perhaps the most dangerous thing a woman can do to a man," Wynstan said with a note of amusement in his voice, "is to make him believe that he is invincible and indefatigable."

He glanced for a moment at Larina's wide eyes and added:

"It is also the best thing she can do; for most men need to have someone to believe in them because they are afraid to believe in themselves."

"I believe in you," Larina said impulsively.

"In what way?" he asked.

"I think you will always get what you want in life. I think too that what you want is something which will help other people and will be of real importance."

She was not really certain of what she was saying, but the words came to her.

There was a silence after she had spoken. Then Wynstan said:

"Thank you, Larina, you have made up my mind for me on a rather important subject."

They said no more because Wynstan seemed to be concentrating on the boat, and once again there was a squall of rain which forced Larina to keep her head down.

It was late afternoon before they finally reached the private jetty of the Villa as they had been crawling along at less than three knots.

The mechanic was waiting for them and Wynstan told him what had happened. While he was exclaiming in dismay at what had occurred, Larina began to climb up the steps towards the Villa.

It was difficult to walk in her soaked skirts

and Wynstan soon caught up with her.

"You need a hot bath," he said firmly, "but first a drink!"

He drew her, although she protested, into a room where there was a tray of drinks set out on a side-table.

"I am ruining the carpet!" she protested.

"Better that than having pneumonia!" he answered. "Drink this — every drop of it!"

It was cognac and Larina felt it sear its way like fire down her throat, but because Wynstan had ordered her to drink it she did so.

Then she went upstairs to where a maid was already drawing her bath, and having taken off her wet clothes she lay soaking in it for a long time.

Then there was her hair to dry, and it was hours later before she came downstairs in evening dress to find Wynstan in the room that she had learnt was usually used in the winter.

It had an open fireplace, and now there was a log-fire burning brightly and a table set in front of it.

Wynstan rose to his feet as she entered the room.

"If you are not hungry — I am!"

Larina smiled at him a little shyly.

Now that she was back in the Villa it was

difficult not to think of how he had kissed her.

She thought about it while she was lying in her bath and told herself that she must not attach too much importance to it.

It was just because he was so pleased with himself at having repaired the engine that he had to express his joy with someone, and she had been standing there beside him.

It had been a revelation to her, but she was sure that to him it had been nothing more than if he had hugged her as a man might hug a child or swing her round in his arms.

The servants appeared with delicious dishes and Larina found that she was in fact very hungry.

"Do you realise it is after seven o'clock?" Wynstan asked. "It is a long time since breakfast, and I suppose, as this must count as dinner, our luncheon is lost forever!"

"I shall not miss it," Larina smiled. "I have never eaten as much as I have done since I came here."

"I had been looking forward to giving you luncheon at Ischia," he said, "but we will go there another day. Tomorrow we will be more cautious and only go the three miles to Capri. Then if we break down again, there will be plenty of people about to rescue us."

"I am not afraid," Larina said.

"Do you want me to tell you how well you behaved?" he asked. "Any other woman would have whined and complained, and many would have been really frightened."

"I was only frightened at first because I was afraid I might be sea-sick," Larina confessed, "and that would have been undignified."

"And very unromantic!" he said.

She thought for a moment that his eyes rested on her lips and she blushed.

He insisted on her drinking wine at dinner and also having a liqueur afterwards.

Then he made her put her legs up on the big velvet sofa which stood in front of the fire and covered her with a fur rug.

"I am not cold now," Larina said.

"I am still afraid you might catch a chill," he replied. "The Mediterranean can be very treacherous at times and very misleading. It changes its moods as quickly as any woman!"

"Are we all so temperamental?" Larina enquired.

"Most woman are," he answered, "but that is what makes them so attractive. If they were always the same I have a feeling it would become very boring."

Larina smiled and snuggled back

amongst the silk cushions.

"I am too tired and too contented to throw a temperament just to amuse you," she said, "but remind me tomorrow to be unpredictable about something or other."

She was speaking lightly, but as she said the word 'tomorrow' once again the question was there.

Would she be with him tomorrow to be unpredictable, or anything else?

"What is worrying you?" Wynstan asked.

"How do you know I am worried?" Larina replied evasively.

"Your eyes are very expressive. I have never known a woman whose expression changes so quickly, or whose eyes are so revealing."

He bent forward in his chair.

"Tell me what it is that frightens you, Larina," he begged. "I know there is something and I cannot bear to see the fear in your eyes."

For a moment she hesitated and then she said:

"I will tell you tomorrow night."

"Is that a promise?" Wynstan asked.

"I . . . promise!"

She thought as she spoke that by tomorrow night he would understand and there would be no need for her to tell him what was wrong — he would know!

It was very comfortable on the sofa, the fire was warm and the liqueur Wynstan had made her drink made her feel as if she were floating on a cloud.

She must have fallen asleep because she was wakened by Wynstan saying:

"You are tired. You were up very early this morning, and nothing could be more exhausting than what we went through today. It is time you went to bed."

"No . . . I want to stay . . . here," Larina protested drowsily.

"I am going to have to make you do as you are told," he answered. "If you feel too tired to walk, I will carry you."

He pulled back the rug as he spoke and picked Larina up in his arms before she could protest.

"Why should you not be 'borne upward on the wings of my human vigour'?" he asked with a smile.

She gave a little chuckle and put her head against his shoulder.

It was a happiness she had never known to be held close in his arms, and she knew that she was so light that it was no effort for him to carry her across the Hall and up the broad staircase which led to her bed-room.

He pushed open the door with his foot.

Then as he entered the room he saw that her eyes were closed and that she had fallen asleep against his shoulder.

Very gently he put her down on the bed.

She opened her eyes as he did so and gave a little murmur as if she minded leaving the security of his arms.

"Shall I call one of the maids?" he asked.

"No," she answered with an effort, "I . . . will manage."

"I have a feeling that as soon as my back is turned you will fall asleep again. So, because I want you to have a good night, Larina, I will turn my back while you undress; then when you are in bed, I will tuck you up."

She looked at him drowsily as he pulled her to her feet and undid the back of her gown with expert fingers.

"Hurry," he said with laughter in his voice, "otherwise I shall find you asleep on the floor!"

He walked away from her as he spoke and pulled aside one of the curtains to look out to sea.

The rain had stopped, but the clouds still hid the stars and there was no moon.

The lights of Naples were twinkling in the distance and Wynstan stood looking at them until a soft voice behind him said:

"I am in . . . bed now."

He turned and walked back to the bed which was draped in frilled muslin.

Larina's hair was golden against the white of the pillows.

He saw that she was wearing a muslin nightgown with long sleeves trimmed with lace which fell over her hands, and with a lace-trimmed collar which fastened at the neck.

He pulled the sheet up to her chin, then he bent his head and kissed her very gently on the lips.

"Good-night, Larina," he said softly.

"Good-night . . . Apollo . . ." she murmured and her eyes closed before she had said the last word.

Wynstan stood looking at her for a long moment; then he turned out the light and went from the room.

Chapter Seven

Larina awoke to find the maid pulling back the curtains.

"What time is it?" she asked sleepily.

"It is half past nine, *signorina,*" the maid replied, "and I thought you would like your breakfast."

"Breakfast!" Larina exclaimed and sat up in bed.

She was dismayed to find that she had slept so long.

She had meant to get up early and see for the last time the dawn breaking, but now by sleeping she had lost some of the precious hours of her last day on earth.

She was angry with herself, and yet at the same time she felt an uncontrollable surge of excitement at the thought of seeing Wynstan again.

Now she remembered that he had carried her up to bed, and although she had been half-asleep she was quite certain that he kissed her before he left the room.

Only to think of the kiss he had given her when they were on the boat was to feel an exquisite ecstasy shoot through her body with a sensation she had never known or even imagined existed.

She had been wet and cold, and yet at that moment she felt as if she glowed like a light with the wonder of his lips.

It had no longer been a grey, wet day, the world seemed brilliant as if Apollo himself had touched it with his fingers.

"That is how I would like to die," Larina told herself and remembered how Homer had written:

'Make the sky clear, and grant us to
  see with our eyes.
In the light be it, although thou
  slayest me.'

"The light! That is what I must find even though I am slain," Larina told herself.

The maid brought her breakfast on a tray on which there rested a white rose.

It smelt delicious and as she held it to her nose Larina told herself that what was left of her life must be happy.

She must not let Wynstan be aware of her apprehension and her fear.

She would try to laugh with him, be gay; then when the moment came he would be there and perhaps she would not mind dying because she would not be alone.

She ate quickly, then walked down the marble steps into the warm bath the maid had prepared for her.

She wondered if any previous occupants of the Villa had ever faced, as she was doing, the knowledge that their life was over and their existence was coming to a full-stop.

"I must not think about it," Larina told herself, "or Wynstan will guess that something is worrying me."

She felt a sudden warmth because he was concerned for her, because last night he wanted her to tell him her secret. She had promised to do so, knowing that she would not have to say it in words, that what happened would speak for itself.

'Will he mind?' she wondered. 'Will he care?'

Then she told herself she was being ridiculous.

Why should he care for her when he had only known her for such a short time?

He had been charming and kind, but it was because he was habitually like that, and although he had kissed her he had also kissed the attractive Italian Contessa.

"Which gown will you wear, *Signorina?*" the maid enquired.

There was one gown which she had not yet worn, one she had bought at Poiret's.

It was white, trimmed with fine lace and slotted through with turquoise-blue ribbons, and a sash of the same colour encircled her waist.

She thought it was the prettiest day-gown she had ever seen in her life and almost instinctively, she thought now, she had kept it for her last day.

She brushed her hair until it shone, then swept it back from her forehead and coiled it low in the back of her neck.

"The *Signorina* is very beautiful! *Bellissima!*"

"Thank you!" Larina replied, feeling the words spoken with obvious sincerity were just what she needed.

She went downstairs and, despite her eagerness to reach Wynstan, she was feeling a little shy.

She found him in the Drawing-Room, seated at the desk writing a letter.

He rose when she appeared and she was sure that he looked at her admiringly.

"I am ashamed of having slept so late," she said.

"You had every reason to be tired."

"What are we . . . going to . . . do today?"

The question was breathless simply because it was so important, and she was afraid he might have changed his plans.

"I promised I would take you to Capri," Wynstan answered, "unless you are afraid to trust yourself again in my badly behaved motor-boat? The mechanic informs me that we can go for miles, and even years, without a recurrence of what happened yesterday!"

"I am not afraid," Larina answered, "and I have wished so much to see Capri."

"Then your wish shall be granted!" Wynstan said. "If you are ready we may as well start right away."

Larina looked up at him excitedly.

She had brought her hat downstairs, and when they reached the Hall Wynstan picked up a blue sun-shade which was lying on a table.

"This belonged to my sister-in-law," he said, "and I think it would be wise to take it with us. It can be very hot on Capri, even though we can try to find somewhere shady under the olive trees."

Larina looked at him enquiringly and he explained:

"I thought today we would have a picnic. I want to go to the south of the island where, as far as I know, there are no restaurants. So the Chef has filled the basket with what he thinks we should eat and drink on such a beautiful island!"

"Then of course it will be ambrosia and

nectar!" Larina smiled.

"Naturally!" Wynstan replied. "What else would the gods consider to be palatable fare?"

They descended the cliff followed by one of the servants carrying the wicker baskets.

The mechanic was waiting for them and assured Wynstan that everything was in order and another break-down was impossible.

"I hope you are right, and thank you!" Wynstan said in fluent Italian.

The servant stowed the picnic away in the cabin.

Wynstan started up the engine and they set off moving at a very different speed from that at which they had limped home the day before.

Today the sea was calm without even a ripple of a wave, and already the sun was blindingly golden and very hot.

Capri was only three miles from the promontory of Sorrento.

As they left it behind Larina looked back and thought how right Ulysses had been to build a Temple to Athene on the outermost point.

"I know what you are thinking," Wynstan said with a smile, "but there were also many Temples on Capri when the Greeks settled there."

"Of course," Larina murmured.

"When Caesar Augustus saw Capri," Wynstan went on, "he was so struck by its beauty that he acquired it from the City of Naples in exchange for Ischia."

He saw that she was listening attentively and he said:

"Tiberius, who came after him, built twelve Villas dedicated to the twelve divinities of Olympus."

"Do any of them still exist?" Larina asked.

"One, at any rate, is in the process of being excavated," Wynstan replied, "but it is going to be too hot for us to do very much sight-seeing. I am afraid you will have to be content with the beauty of the island."

There was no doubt that it was beautiful.

As they drew nearer Larina saw that its high mountains, the highest being Mt. Salerno, seemed almost blue, a mystical, entrancing blue that she felt must somehow belong to the gods.

They passed the Marina Grande, the main harbour, and proceeded round the high sharp cliffs.

Wynstan pointed out to her various grottos that he said she must explore another day.

Then with the sea vividly blue, the

dolomitic cliffs rising perpendicularly out of it, cut and tunnelled by time into fantastic shapes, they came to the south of the island.

Here there was a small harbour beside a natural formation of rock jutting into the sea.

"This is the Marina Piccola where we leave the boat and climb," Wynstan explained. "I am afraid there is no road and no carriage, so I hope you are feeling energetic?"

"I am!" Larina answered.

"High above this Marina are the gardens of Augustus," Wynstan told her. "I warn you — it is a steep climb!"

"I am not afraid."

They tied up the boat, then Wynstan carried the wicker baskets and they set out to climb from the little beach up the side of the cliffs.

There was a path, narrow and twisting, and it was not too difficult but Larina was glad of the sunshade as the sun beat down on their heads.

Finally they found at the top of the path trees, grass and a profusion of wild flowers of every colour.

"I think we have gone high enough," Wynstan said.

As he spoke Larina gave a little cry.

She could see some ruins, two arches worn by time and the weather, which had obviously at one time been part of a building.

"Is that the Villa of Augustus?" she asked.

"It is," Wynstan replied, "and you can imagine him coming here to rest, and planning where else the Romans could extend their Empire, and perhaps too deciding how he could extort more money and more slaves from the races he had conquered!"

"Do not spoil it for me," Larina begged. "I want to think of people being happy on this beautiful island."

It was, she thought, more beautiful than she could ever have imagined. The vivid blue of the Mediterranean which reflected the blue of the sky seemed to intensify the green of the grass and the flowers which filled it.

Wynstan found a comfortable place near a tree where he set down the wicker baskets.

Then he half-laid down on the ground supporting himself on his elbow.

"Come and join me," he said to Larina as she stood looking out to sea. "We can pretend we are Romans, or Greeks, if you prefer and the world, or what has been discovered of it, will be well lost in exchange for this little Paradise on its own."

'That is exactly what it is,' Larina thought.

She did as Wynstan suggested and sat down beside him, shutting her sun-shade and taking off her hat.

Wynstan watched her.

"You are Greek!" he declared and after a moment: "Pure Greek with your straight little nose and your hair which seems to hold the sunshine."

"There is no need for me to return the compliment!"

"Last night you called me Apollo!"

She felt the colour come into her face and dropped her eyes.

"I was asleep," she answered.

"I am not complaining!" he said with a smile, "and if we were Greeks, even quite ordinary Greek people, we should, if we were born at the right time, think of ourselves as creatures shining in a divine light."

"Did they really think that?" Larina asked.

"Their naval victory over the Persians off the Island of Salamis," Wynstan answered, "was so close to being a miracle that the Greeks really believed that the gods had been present, fighting on their side."

"When was that?" Larina enquired.

"On a warm sunny day rather like this,"

Wynstan replied, "in September, 280 B.C."

"And after that, they were free, liberated from the threat of Persian domination?" Larina enquired.

"Completely!" Wynstan replied. "And for fifty years they lived, thought, built Temples, sculpted and painted as if they were the natural children of the gods."

"Why?" Larina asked.

"I believe that their prodigious strength," Wynstan replied slowly, "came from the fact that in some way which we have forgotten or lost they linked up with a divine force which men call 'God' or 'Life'."

"Do you think it is always there if we need it?" Larina asked.

"I am sure of that," Wynstan replied, "and that is why in the space of two generations the Greeks set out to conquer the furthermost regions of the human spirit, and in doing so established an Empire over the mind which has altered the whole course of human thinking right up to the present day."

"Is that really true?" Larina asked.

"Because a divine visitation occurred in Greece," Wynstan answered, "men's minds moved faster, their eyes saw further and their bodies were equipped with unsuspected powers."

"And today?" Larina asked.

"We can still find what the Greeks found — if we try hard enough."

Larina drew in her breath.

"What you are really saying is that we ourselves can tap this power or 'Divine light', and we can not only use it in this world, so that we can become permeated with it but we are part of it when we die?"

It seemed to her as she spoke as if Wynstan had cleared away from her mind everything that had been worrying her, everything she had not understood.

There was silence, then he said:

"Blake wrote: 'Where others see but the dawn coming over the hill, I see the Sons of God shouting for joy'!"

He smiled at Larina as he went on:

"The Greeks regarded themselves as the sons of God and the echo of their joyful shouting can be heard down the ages. We can do the same!"

"That is what I want to do," Larina said. "I think it is what I have always wanted but now you have made it clear."

"It is Capri which makes it clearer than anywhere else outside Greece itself," Wynstan said.

He lay down on his back and looked at the branches of the trees above him.

"Here it is easy to believe," he said, "away from the sounds of traffic and machinery, away from the overpowering height and size of sky-scrapers! Men's buildings belittle themselves."

"I know what you mean," Larina said.

There was no need to put into words that the translucent light, the blue, limpid glow of the island, was so exquisite and so serene she felt as if she could leap either into the sky or into the sea and be no longer herself but a part of them.

Here in Capri the mind could soar free, and there were no longer any problems or fear, but only beauty.

They were silent, and yet it was a close sort of silence which made Larina feel almost as if Wynstan touched her.

Then after a long time he said:

"I do not know about you, but I am hungry! I had breakfast very early."

"That is what I meant to do," Larina said, "and I was angry with myself for over-sleeping."

"We will make it up," Wynstan said lightly. "Why not open the baskets and see if there is anything to eat?"

Larina did as she was told, then laughed.

"There is enough food here for a whole army!" she exclaimed.

"There is nothing Italians enjoy more than arranging a picnic," Wynstan replied.

He was busy as he spoke opening a bottle of golden wine.

"It should really be cooler," he said. "The one thing that is sometimes lacking on Capri is water. Yet strangely enough, or perhaps through divine influence, the vineyards, orange-groves and gardens are highly productive. I have always been told there are more variations of flowers and shrubs here than anywhere else in Italy."

He poured some of the wine into two glasses and held one out for Larina.

"Drink it slowly," he said, "and imagine it is nectar. Even if the gods have a purer taste, I think I shall find it palatable."

Larina did as she was told.

"It is delicious!" she exclaimed.

"That is what I thought," Wynstan smiled.

She spread out on the grass all that the Chef had packed for them.

There was a fish pâté so light and so smooth it seemed to melt in the mouth. There were slices of ham cut fine as a pocket handkerchief, and small *Neapolitan dolci* known as *Sfogliatelle* made of baked pastry and filled with such delicious and novel ingredients that it was difficult to guess what they contained.

There were black olives exactly ripe because Italians think those are important to any meal, and there were *Crocchette di Patate* or croquettes which Wynstan said were a great favourite in Naples and consisted of potatoes and Parmesan cheese rolled in fine breadcrumbs and fried in oil.

Besides these there were a number of local cheeses and one speciality *Prouola di pecora* from the Sorrentine district which was made from ewe's milk.

They were all delicious, and afterwards there were peaches which Wynstan insisted on peeling for her and putting in a glass of white wine, and there were figs and walnuts, another speciality of Sorrento.

There was coffee in a flask which had kept it warm and which Wynstan enjoyed more than Larina.

"That is better!" he exclaimed.

"Much better!" Larina agreed. "But the trouble is that now I feel lazy and not half so eager to explore the island as I was before we started luncheon!"

She packed what was left of the food, with the knives, forks and glasses back into the picnic baskets. Then she looked rather doubtfully at Wynstan who was lying back amongst the grass as he had done before the meal.

"I feel that we should start off at once and see the rest of Capri," she said tentatively.

"It is too hot," he replied. "No sensible Italian ever hurries about at this time of the day. Lie down for a few moments, Larina. A *siesta* is good for the soul as well as the body."

Because she had no wish to go off exploring alone Larina did as he suggested.

Lying full length on the soft grass she was conscious of the fragrance of the flowers, the smell of freshness, as if everything was young and untouched.

"That is better!" Wynstan said approvingly. "I do not like busy women!"

"Is that what I am?"

"No. You have a serenity about you which I like and envy."

"Just as I envy you."

"Why should you do that?"

He raised himself on his elbow as he spoke and looked down at her.

Now she could see his head silhouetted against the branches of the trees and the sunlight coming through them seeming to envelop him with an aura of light.

"I envy you," she said, "because you seem so sure of yourself and you have so much more to do in the world."

Wynstan did not answer.

Then she realised he was looking down at

her and she felt shy of the expression in his eyes. Suddenly he said:

"You are lovely! Lovelier than anyone I have ever seen before!"

As he spoke his lips found hers and it seemed to her as if he swooped down from the sky and took possession of her.

For a moment his kiss was gentle and her mouth was very soft beneath his. Then as his lips grew more demanding, more insistent, she felt herself quiver with the ecstasy that she had known before, though now it was more insistent, more divine.

It was as if a light invaded her whole being, infusing it with a strange glow and a wonder that was indescribable.

She felt as if everything beautiful around them was in the feeling Wynstan gave her. The blue of the sea and sky, the mystery of the island, the flowers and the very leaves of the trees were all part of the wonder of herself and him.

There was nothing in the whole world but Wynstan. He filled the Universe and she no longer had any identity of her own.

Finally he raised his head a little to say:

"My darling, I cannot resist you! You have enslaved me from the moment I first saw you in the Temple and thought you were Aphrodite!"

"I thought . . . you were . . . Apollo!" Larina whispered.

She could hardly speak, it was hard to do anything but thrill with a pulsating wonder because he had kissed her.

"What more could either of us ask?" Wynstan enquired.

Then he was kissing her again, kissing her mouth, her eyes, her forehead, her small straight nose, her cheeks, her ears, then her mouth again.

For Larina there was no time, there was only a glory which blinded, dazzled and be-witched her until she could no longer think.

Later Wynstan undid the muslin bow she wore round her neck so that he could kiss the rounded softness of it.

It made her quiver with a new sensation she had not felt before and now the breath came quickly between her lips and her eye-lids felt a little heavy, although she was not sleepy . . .

"How can anyone be so beautiful?" he asked a long time later, tracing the outline of her forehead with his finger down the straightness of her nose, over her lips and under her chin.

"Your face is perfect!" he went on. "I knew when I first saw you that I had seen you in my mind when I first looked at the statue of Aphrodite in the Temple."

"I had been thinking of Apollo all day," Larina said, "and I was thinking as the sun went down that it was Apollo taking the light to the other side of the world and leaving me in darkness. Then I turned and you were there!"

"If I had done what I knew instinctively I should do," Wynstan said, "I should have taken you in my arms. There would have been no need for explanations, no need to get to know each other. We knew already!"

Then he was kissing her again, kissing her until she moved nearer to stir against him, her whole body seeming to ache with a strange feeling that she could not understand.

"I love you! I love you!" he said over and over again. "I have been looking for you all my life. Every beautiful woman I have met has disappointed me because she was not you!"

He kissed her small chin and the corners of her mouth as he continued:

"There was always something missing, something I could not put into words, but which my heart missed."

"Is that why you have never married?" Larina asked.

Even as she said the word she felt as though she had thrown a stone into the water and the ripples from it spread out and multiplied.

There was silence, then Wynstan said:

"I have never asked a woman to marry me, until now. You have secrets from me, Larina — secrets you have promised to tell me tonight. I do not mind what they are. Whatever you have done or whatever you are hiding, it is of no consequence."

His arms tightened.

"Our spirits have found each other. You are everything my heart has been looking for and that is all that matters."

He bent his head again and now he was kissing her more passionately, more fiercely than he had done before.

He kissed her until she felt as if the ground was insubstantial beneath her, and the sky moved dizzily overhead.

He kissed her until it was no longer possible to breathe and she felt as if her whole body glowed with a strange light.

"I love you! I love you!" he was saying and she heard her own voice tremulous, and yet lilting with an inexplicable joy reply:

"I love . . . you! Oh, Apollo . . . I love . . . you!"

He kissed her again and again, then his

lips were on her neck evoking the strange sensations he had done before.

Quite suddenly Larina thought this is how she must die, close to Wynstan when she belonged to him and she was his. There would be no fear and no suffering in his arms.

"I love you!" he said again.

"Will you not . . . love me completely," she whispered, "as a man loves a woman and makes her . . . his. I want to . . . belong to you . . . to be yours!"

Her voice died away because she realised that Wynstan was suddenly still.

He seemed to stiffen and she knew in that moment that what she had said was wrong! It had raised a barrier between them and she could have cried out at the misery of it.

Slowly he raised himself, then without speaking he rose to his feet to walk a little way from her and look down at the sea.

Larina sat up.

She had made a mistake, she had lost him and it was an inexpressible agony, like a knife turning in her heart.

He stood there for what seemed to be a long time and she watched him apprehensively also without moving.

Finally he seemed to give a deep sigh which came from the very depths of his being.

"I think we have to go back," he said.

"There are a lot of things we have to talk about and I do not want to keep you out in the dark."

Larina wanted to protest! She wanted to run towards him and say she did not mean it, to ask him to kiss her again, to feel the closeness and warmth of him, but somehow the words would not come to her lips.

There was nothing she could do but pick up her hat and sun-shade.

Wynstan moved towards the picnic baskets and now she did not look at him but started the descent towards the Marina below them.

As she went she was vividly conscious of his footsteps following her.

The sun was no longer as strong as it had been during the afternoon and Larina knew it was growing late.

Everything still had that transparent luminance and once they were in the boat she could see that the mountains above the cliffs were even more blue than they had been before.

Wynstan drove the boat speedily, but while they were rounding the island Larina had plenty of time in which to wonder miserably how she could explain to him, how she could make him understand why she had said what she had.

'Perhaps I shall be dead before we reach the Villa,' she thought.

But everything within her cried out at the idea that she should die without Wynstan's lips on hers, without his arms around her.

It was impossible to speak intimately above the noise of the engine and yet every second that passed, it seemed to Larina, might make it too late to explain, too late to make him understand.

They rounded the south point and when Larina thought Wynstan would head straight for Sorrento he turned towards her with a smile and said:

"We have missed our English tea. I think perhaps before we set out on the last part of our journey we might stop at the Marina Grande and have some oysters. What do you think?"

Because he was speaking kindly to her again, because there was a smile on his face, Larina would have agreed to anything.

"That would be . . . lovely!" she cried.

"And they have clams and very large prawns which I am sure you would enjoy if you have never tried them," he said conversationally.

She felt as if he had deliberately set aside what had upset him and perhaps puzzled him.

He was being as kind and charming to her as he had been on the outward voyage.

Although she longed for the deep note in his voice when he said he loved her, although she wanted to see again the expression in his eyes which had told her he spoke the truth, she was content for the moment.

He wanted to talk to her and at any rate he seemed not actually angry.

"How could I have suggested anything so . . . immodest, so . . . wrong and . . . wicked?" Larina asked herself accusingly.

It had just been a moment of desperation because she had known there were perhaps only a few hours or a few seconds left, and she loved Wynstan with all her heart and soul and more than her hope of eternity.

Nothing mattered except him! Nothing existed in the whole world except his lips!

"He will . . . understand when I am . . . dead," she told herself miserably.

She watched him, her eyes on his profile, knowing that to her he was perfect. Even if he were angry with her it would only make her love him more.

They reached the Marina Grande. Wynstan entered the harbour and brought the motor-boat up against the jetty.

The sun was shining and now the white buildings all along the water's edge were diffused with colours — crimson and gold.

Behind them, the green mountains with their bare tops also glowed as if from a fire and the sea shimmered with it.

"I will tell you what I will do," Wynstan said. "I will go and fetch the oysters and whatever else there is for us to eat. You set the table in the cabin."

"I will do that," Larina agreed, glad to have something with which to occupy her mind.

Then as Wynstan was ready to step ashore she said:

"You will . . . not be long?"

"No," he answered, "the restaurant where one buys the oysters is quite near. I shall not be more than a few minutes."

There were a number of small boys on the Quay only too willing to help tie up the boat. They stared at it excitedly, pointing out the wheel and the engine and chattering amongst themselves.

Larina went into the cabin. She found a cloth of gay red and white checks with which she covered the table.

In the same drawer were knives, forks and glasses which she arranged while all the while her mind was on Wynstan.

Finding there was a mirror in the cabin she smoothed her hair and retied the little muslin bow at her neck which he had undone and which she had replaced hastily with trembling fingers before they had started the descent to the boat.

In the mirror Larina could see her eyes very large in her pale face.

'Oh, God . . . make him . . . understand,' she prayed. 'I love him! I love him so desperately! Make him understand and . . . love me again before I . . . die."

Wynstan found to his satisfaction that the restaurant he had known ever since he first came to Sorrento was still in existence.

It was famous for its fish, but most especially for its oysters, clams and mussels.

There were fish swimming in tanks of water outside the door, and as a boy he had found it amusing to choose what he wanted to eat and watch the waiter catch it in a small net.

He entered the restaurant and gave his order for an *arogosta*-lobster which already cooked was lying on a green salad garnished with prawns.

"The Signor must try our *Zuppa di cozze*," the proprietor suggested.

Wynstan knew this was a soup made from mussels which was a speciality of the restaurant.

"Will it take long?" he asked.

"Five minutes, *Signor,* and I will serve it in a covered dish so that you can take it to your boat, as long as you promise to bring back the dish!"

"I will do that," Wynstan answered. "Very well then, I will have the *Zuppa di cozze* and two dozen *Ostriche*-oysters. Open them and in the meantime, I will take the lobster and the wine back with me now."

They were being packed into an open basket and Wynstan was waiting to leave the restaurant when he heard a voice he recognised.

"Wynstan! What are you doing here?"

It was Nicole, surrounded as usual by men and looking extremely attractive.

"As you see," Wynstan answered, "I am shopping."

"It sounds very domestic," she smiled, "but I will not ask awkward questions. I am well aware that you could not eat all that yourself."

"Hello, Wynstan," the man who had joined her remarked.

Wynstan held out his hand.

"Hello, Chuck," he said. "I have not seen you in ages."

"I arrived this morning. Nicole told me you were in Sorrento and I had hoped we could get together and talk over old times."

"I hope so," Wynstan replied automatically.

"By the way," Chuck said, "I was sorry to hear about your brother, but he really had not much chance against Roosevelt."

"Roosevelt has been re-elected?" Wynstan asked. "I expected it!"

"Yes, he is back in the White House," Chuck said. "If you want to read about it I have yesterday's newspaper which I brought with me from Rome."

"Thank you," Wynstan said.

"Do come on, Chuck," Nicole interposed, "you know we have people for dinner and we shall be late if you do not hurry."

She paused to say to Wynstan:

"Join us if you feel like it. You know I want to see you."

"I am afraid I shall be too late," Wynstan replied.

She had received his note, he thought, and she was really behaving quite sensibly about it.

"Here is the newspaper," Chuck said.

He handed it to Wynstan and hurried after Nicole who, with the two other men in the party, was already walking towards the jetty.

Wynstan picked up the rest of his purchases

254

but gave them time to move away in a motor-boat which was not as up-to-date as his own and which required two crew to run it.

He then walked back to the 'Napier Minor' and saw Larina smiling at him from the cabin as he stepped aboard.

"Here is the first course, at any rate," he said handing her the wicker basket. "I have to go back for the rest, but I have ordered something which I think you will like."

"It sounds exciting!" Larina replied.

"You will enjoy the *Zuppa di cozze*," Wynstan promised. "I will not be long."

He walked away again back towards the restaurant.

Larina carried the basket into the cabin. She put it down on one of the bunks, saw there was a newspaper on top of it, and laid it on the table.

Then she lifted out the lobster and thought how prettily arranged it was on the dish. There were also two bottles of wine, fresh rolls and a small china pot containing butter!

As Larina looked at the lobster she realised that she was in fact not hungry.

She had felt ever since she had upset Wynstan that there was a constriction in her throat, and something suspiciously like a stone heavy in her breast.

Because she could not bear for the moment to think about herself or how foolish she had been, she opened the paper.

It was an American paper, published in Rome, but printed in English.

ROOSEVELT BACK AS PRESIDENT

Larina read the headlines and wondered if Wynstan was interested in politics. He had never mentioned them, and yet, she thought, if there had been a General Election in England, people would have talked of little else.

She looked further down the page, then suddenly she gave a shrill cry like an animal that had been wounded.

It seemed to echo round the small cabin. Then with a violent gesture, she threw the paper onto the floor and climbing out of the boat onto the jetty, started to run frantically — wildly!

Wynstan had to wait longer than he had expected for the *Zuppa di cozze*.

"It is coming, *Signor* — one little second!" the proprietor kept assuring him.

The oysters were opened and arranged neatly on a tray so that they were easy to carry.

Finally the *Zuppa di cozze* came from the kitchen and the proprietor told a waiter to carry it to the boat.

The two men set off down the jetty.

By now the sun was very low on the horizon and darkness was encroaching across the sky carrying with it the first faint twinkling stars.

Wynstan glanced up and remembered that the moon would be full tonight, so there would be no difficulty in finding his way back to Sorrento.

There he would talk to Larina and there would be no more secrets between them. He would no longer be apprehensive about what she had to tell him.

He knew he had hurt her, he knew he had brought her back, from an ecstasy that had seemed to them both divine, to the mundane and the common-place.

Yet he had not been able to prevent his feelings about something which concerned Elvin.

He had to know! He had to hear what it was that had worried and perturbed her ever since he had known her and which had made her send that frantic telegram across the Atlantic.

He and the waiter reached the boat.

There was no sign of Larina and Wynstan

thought she was perhaps lying down on one of the bunks inside.

He put the tray with the oysters on the flat roof of the cabin and took the soup from the waiter, tipping him as he did so.

"Grazie, Signor," the waiter said and hurried back towards the restaurant.

"Here I am, Larina?" Wynstan called out, "with our culinary feast!"

He bent his head and entered the cabin as he spoke to set the deep dish containing the soup down on the table.

To his surprise Larina was not there!

'She must have gone for a walk,' he thought.

He collected the tray from the roof of the cabin and put that too on the table. Then he went outside again.

There was no sign of her on the jetty and it surprised him that she could have walked towards the harbour without his seeing her.

He swung himself out of the boat and started to walk slowly back the way he had come from the restaurant.

'Where can she be?' he wondered.

There were no shops by the water's edge to interest a woman and now the sun had almost vanished and the dusk was purple in the shadows.

Wynstan reached the Quay and looked around him.

The restaurants and the cafes were already bright with light, but there were not many people about and the small boys had gone home for their supper.

A few fishermen were getting their boats ready for the morning, but otherwise it was very quiet. He thought perhaps he had made a mistake: Larina must in fact have been at the end of the jetty and he had not seen her.

He walked back to the boat.

Everything was as he had left it and there was no sign of her.

He wondered where on earth she could have gone to. In spite of what she had said to him yesterday she had never seemed to be unpredictable, but always easy and pliable, and in that aspect different from any other woman he had ever known.

He decided she would not be long and he might as well open the wine.

He found a corkscrew, drew the cork from one of the bottles and sampled it. It was good, although it did not compare with the wine they drank at the Villa, most of which had been put down in his grandfather's time and was exceptional.

He came out of the cabin and stood in the front of the boat. It was not easy to see far in the gathering dusk, but there was still no sign of Larina.

Her dress was white and he knew he would have seen it long before he would notice any other colour.

Puzzled he went back to the cabin again.

It was then his eye alighted on the newspaper lying on the floor.

The way it was unfolded and thrown down told him that Larina must have read it.

He picked it up and saw the headline.

ROOSEVELT BACK AS PRESIDENT

She could hardly be upset about that, he thought, unless there was something in the report. He read it hastily.

It told him that Harvey had won a number of votes though not enough. There was nothing that could have disturbed Larina or lead her to associate the election in any way with him.

Then his eye caught a paragraph low down on the page headed — London.

He read it automatically hardly realising he was doing so.

MAD DOCTOR IMPERSONATES ROYAL CONSULTANT.

George Robson, a Doctor, who last year was struck off the Medical Register for unprofessional conduct, was arrested in London today and charged with impersonating Sir John Coleridge, Consultant to the Royal family.

Sir John, who was on holiday abroad, left his house in Wimpole Street in charge of a caretaker. George Robson, who had a particular grudge against Sir John because he was on the Board of the B.M.A. who had condemned him in 1899, gained access to No. 55 Wimpole Street. He imprisoned the caretaker in a downstairs room where he subsequently strangled him, and dressed in borrowed clothes, proceeded to interview any patients who called to see Sir John or who endeavoured to make appointments.

Robson was clever enough to see only patients who had not previously been examined and would therefore not recognise Sir John. The masquerade was only discovered when Sir John returned from his holiday four days earlier than he had intended.

George Robson had in fact left 55 Wimpole Street the previous day. Sir John was confronted with an angry patient who had obtained a second opinion on his condition. It was then discovered that every patient who had been seen by George Robson in the last month had been given exactly twenty-one days to live.

He told them they had a strange and unusual condition of the heart, that he was an authority on the disease and there was no hope of their survival. Sir John is trying to contact all the patients who might have been interviewed by George Robson, but as there is no record of how many people Robson saw, it will of course take some time.

Wynstan read the report at first quickly and then slowly for the second time. He realised that here must be the explanation of everything which had puzzled him, everything which Larina had kept secret.

Now he knew he must find her quickly.

He jumped out of the boat and ran down to the jetty.

It was obvious when he reached the Quay that she would turn right because there were fewer houses that way and almost immediately there was a road rising up the hill.

He walked up it, but when it turned at a right angle it seemed to him that she would not have carried on to where there were other houses and shops, but would have taken to the mountainside.

There was a path, narrow and twisting but he knew he had to trust his instinct, and he was almost sure this was the way she would have gone.

He set off looking around him and feeling thankful, as the sun sank and the stars came out, that there was also moonlight.

It was not bright at first but it grew brighter. There was not a cloud in the sky and soon the island was bathed in a silver light, ethereal and compelling.

Soon Wynstan had climbed above the olive-trees and grotesque, twisting rocks rose abruptly in front of him.

He still climbed, looking everywhere for something white, something he knew would show even against the rocks and stones which gave back a dull reflection of the moonlight.

It must have been two hours later that he saw Larina, below him instead of above, a patch of brilliant white against the lesser white of the stone on which she sat.

He started to make his way down to her and realised she was crouched on the ground, her head bent, her face hidden in her hands.

Now there was no urgency, no hurry and

he came towards her slowly and quietly so as not to frighten her.

He stood for a moment looking down at her, her attitude one of poignant despair. Then he knelt beside her and put his arms around her.

He felt her quiver convulsively.

"It is all right, my darling!" he said. "I understand."

For a moment he thought she would resist him, then she hid her head against his shoulder.

"It is all right!" he said again. "There is nothing more of which you need be afraid. It is all over!"

He realised as he spoke that she was very cold with shock and also from the night air, which was chilly when one was not moving.

He pulled her to her feet and picked her up in his arms.

She made a little murmur as if of dissent, then she put one arm round his neck and hid her face again.

Afterwards Wynstan used to wonder how he had managed to carry Larina sure-footedly over the rough ground, down the steep paths — little more than sheep-tracks — that twisted and turned their way from the hill to the Quay.

But he had never slipped, and he seldom faltered.

Finally he reached the boat and carrying Larina aboard, he took her into the cabin and set her down on one of the bunks.

There was a cushion for her head but when he wanted her to lie against it she gave a little cry of dissent and her arm tightened around his neck.

"I want to give you something to drink, my sweet," he said.

It was then she began to cry: hard, broken sobs which shook her whole body.

He held her very close, cradling her against him as if she were a child, and murmuring soft endearments as she wept.

"It is all right, my sweet, my darling, my precious little Aphrodite. You are not going to die! You are going to live! There is nothing to be unhappy about — nothing to worry you any more!"

Larina's sobs began to abate and finally Wynstan took out his handkerchief to wipe her closed eyes and the tears which had run down her cheeks.

"Why did you not tell me?" he asked at length when she had taken a few sips from the glass of wine he held to her lips.

"E-Elvin had said . . . he would come to me if I ever . . . needed him and if I was dying," Larina answered. "I could not . . . bear to tell . . . anyone else."

"I understand that," Wynstan said, "but Elvin, my precious, is dead!"

"De . . . ad?"

She was very still.

"I was with him when he died," Wynstan went on, "and he said something which now I understand."

He knew she was listening and he continued speaking very quietly:

"Elvin said: 'It is wonderful to be free! Tell . . .' I am sure now he was about to say your name; but if he did, I could not hear it."

Larina drew a deep breath.

"What . . . day did he . . . die?"

"It was on the 23rd March."

"He said he would . . . call me when he was . . . dying."

"Perhaps he was about to do so," Wynstan answered soothingly.

Larina gave a little cry.

"What is it?" he asked.

"The 23rd!" she exclaimed. "I knew . . . I did know! . . . He came to me as he . . . said he would!"

"How?" Wynstan asked.

"What time . . . did he . . . die?"

"About ten o'clock in the morning."

"Is there not . . . five hours difference between New York time and London?"

"Yes, there is."

"Then . . . that was the afternoon! I went to Hyde Park and sat near the Serpentine. Because I was so . . . lonely I called . . . Elvin and he came to me . . . in his own way . . . he came to me."

There was an elation in Larina's voice that was very moving, and as she looked up at Wynstan he saw tears in her eyes — but they were now tears of joy.

"He kept his . . . promise! Only I did not . . . realise that it was he bringing me . . . life and . . . light."

"That is what he found himself," Wynstan said in his deep voice.

"I understand now," Larina said, "and I think . . . he must have . . . sent you to me."

"I am sure he did. But why did you run away?"

She hid her face against him and whispered:

"I am . . . so ashamed . . . of what I . . . suggested."

Wynstan's arms tightened as she went on:

"I am not . . . really sure . . . about what men and women . . . do when they . . . make love . . . but it must be . . . wonderful . . . because the gods used to . . . assume human guise . . ."

Her voice died away.

"It is wonderful, my darling, when two people love each other," Wynstan said.

"I thought . . . I would . . . die . . . while you were . . . loving me."

"I will make love to you, my precious little Aphrodite, but you will not die."

It was like a pattern unfolding before his eyes, he thought. But Larina must never know what Harvey had suspected or what he himself had begun to believe on the journey from New York.

Harvey would never understand what had really happened nor would Gary. But perhaps one day he would be able to tell his mother.

In the meantime he had found Larina and she had found him which was all that mattered. They were together, just as Elvin would have wanted them to be.

His lips were on Larina's forehead as he said:

"Suddenly everything seems very simple, my precious. All the difficulties, all the complications and the secrets have gone!"

"It is like coming out into the light," Larina answered. "I have been afraid . . . so desperately afraid of . . . death and of dying . . . alone."

She gave a deep sigh.

"I shall never be afraid again . . . not even when I really come to . . . die. Elvin has taught me that."

She paused to add shyly:

"And so have . . . you!"

"There is so much for us both to do together before we die," Wynstan said. "You said yesterday that I had work to do in the future which would be of benefit to other people. I think I have found something which will certainly interest me, and I hope, you too."

"What is it?" Larina asked.

"When I was in India, the Viceroy, Lord Curzon, asked me to help him in finding and restoring the magnificent Temples and monuments in India which are being destroyed through neglect. They are a heritage to the world, and if someone does not take the trouble to save them and spend money on them, then they will be lost to posterity."

He kissed Larina's forehead again before he said:

"I think that, darling, is something we can both do together, and what is more we will both find it enthralling."

"Do you . . . really . . . want me?" Larina asked in a low voice.

"I want you more than I can possibly explain in words," he answered. "I want you not only because you are so beautiful, but because for me it is also an aching, spiritual need to have you with me for the rest of our lives."

"That is what I want . . . too," Larina murmured.

"We will be married immediately," Wynstan said. "And we will go for our honeymoon to Greece!"

She gave a little cry of sheer delight and he added:

"Would that make you happy?"

"I can imagine . . . nothing more thrilling," Larina answered, "than to see Greece and to be with . . . Apollo!"

She could hardly say the last words because Wynstan's lips were on hers.

He kissed her passionately, and yet she thought there was something more wonderful, more holy and more sacred in his kiss than there had been before.

It was as if he lifted her up to Olympus where they were both gods.

"I love you!" she heard him say. "God, how I love you!"

Yet somehow his voice seemed very far away and there was only the light — the blinding light of life in which there is no death.